OF THE DEPENDENCE

Charlie Rickle

Contents

Comprehending the Seemingly Impossible Physics Within the Mountains

By Dr. Podgy Atkinson

Dark conifers blanket the mountain, their proud branches strangle the light of the scalding sun, turning day to dusk and night to blindness. There is a life to it that swells with the lungs of the branches, each extension lurching to and fro as the leaves and needles cling on tighter. If there was even more life to it, you could see the knuckles growing paler and paler. Suffocated between some small civilizations, the forests crawl and dig the roots of their trees into the dry soil like nails hooking into plump flesh. And still yet, the civilizations find the spectacle that unfurls along with the existence of the mountains. The impossible mountains. There is no reason why any of it should exist, and yet we are unable to explore it, as humanity is unable to thrive in such conditions. It is as though the venom of the mountains grips anything that could possibly approach it and allows it to singe.

Above, the clouds forecast the withering humanity as though each dark canyon of a blotch is brimming with the bustling conspiracies of the subconscious. They appear almost as flying ashes, their form and color both resembling the utter hopelessness and destruction of a forest fire or volcano. It is as though the blazing white sun casts its turmoil onto unguarded crops, with or without its demanding gaze entrancing the Earth as it twists it around its knuckles.

The gushing river- the arteries leading to the heart of the mountain- evaporate in the day, each droplet scurrying away in fear of the sun, and freeze over in utter cowardice at night, leaving a brief window of hope for any man ill enough to attempt to view the horrors of the mountain himself. Some scientists have speculated that the water flowing in the streams may contain otherworldly properties, as it does not appear to behave in the same manner as normal drinking water. The only portion of the stream safe from the sun and lack thereof resides within the lake in the heart of the forest, where a deep fog dances over the surface of the water. It appears as though it hopes to draw one closer and press his lips against it, anchoring him down- another one claimed like Narcissus- drowning and killing the vicious ego that arises from the journey. One can only imagine the sweet comfort of the stream in this short eclipse of time- the extravaganza of feeling the most satisfying drink running over one's own heart. It is the only justifiable intent.

The surrounding societies have concealed themselves from the global population. The population is lower, and the towns are spread apart like water and oil. Those who live near the mountain are aware of the dangers, but outside of these societies, people are uneducated in reference to its culture. They come for the extravaganza of experiencing a mountain so tall and impossible, but are deaf to the stories and theories that surround it. The same babble over and over slowly fades to the crackle and shuffling of white noise. How unfortunate it is that humanity only wants to hear the voice resonating from its own chest, and fails to take the moment to listen to those who warn against their very curiosities.

Despite the sweltering days and freezing nights, the myths and legends- the looming ambiguity of a creature, the certainty of death looming more reliable than the hood of the pine trees over their shoulders- campers and hikers still persevere to leave a lasting footprint in the falling snow of dusk. The mountains are impossible. I fear this means that the horrors within it may be beyond our comprehension and anticipation.

Chapter One

My dearest love, I had sworn to you that your life would forever come before mine.

A melting sun poured itself into the window reflections, its iterations gluing themselves like candle wax into the irises of those who witnessed it. Soon it would solidify with the sun's absence until it would arise the next morning, only to reheat the rings around it and puddle once again. The temperature ideally dropped just below comfort, warning the family of the changing seasons, but not warranting any extra fabrics to protect them. The occasional breeze would pass by them, rustling the thin hairs on his arms like a passerby in a congregation, each one interrupted and sticking up straight, but barely summoning the bumps that indicated a chill.

Her tricycle had struck the road wrong, perhaps because she had tumbled upon a rock or a crack or because of too much momentum, and it had thrust her over. Her knees skimmed around the pavement, and her palms dragged on the rough concrete. She was at the age where it would take her a moment to contemplate what had just happened to her, but after ruminating long enough, tears overtook her eyes, the remaining dye of the sun magnified within them.

He had not been paying attention until it was too late, and he found himself hurrying to her assistance before his head had even turned entirely. She pressed her face into his chest, the cotton of his shirt sucking up the salted tears in her eyes. He felt a muffled whimper resonate through his body, and he pulled her tighter to himself.

"It'll be fine, Clara," he told her. And then he thought to himself briefly, holding onto it as a promise, but understanding deep down how he could never fulfil it. *I'll never let anything hurt you again.*

***

"Father, it'll be fine!" Clara comforted as she placed a thin hand on his back. The tall man was curled over to half his size, and it made her height more apparent. Her eyes bounced to the clock behind him, hung between dusted frames with sun-bleached photographs and softcover books with fraying edges. She should have left exactly thirteen minutes ago, but Jim's hyperventilation impeded her departure. He held his features in his palms, hiding away any sense of expression she might have been able to extrapolate.

The trek was expected to take three weeks, four if she was unlucky. She was prepared but hoped it wouldn't come down to that. She expected to reach the summit somewhere between week four and five, once again, provided all went to plan. Countless months had been dedicated to proper fitness, dieting, and smaller treks in order to assure she would be able to demonstrate her independence to her father. She wondered about the value of her actions and whether her father would ever be able to let her go, but knew somewhere in the back of her mind that she would most likely be caring for him for the rest of his days. After that, she would be free.

She gently pulled his hands from his face, and although she had known him for the entirety of her life, it felt like it was the first time she had taken a decent glance at him in some time. She hardly noticed that the smiles of her childhood had etched themselves into the stubble of her father, and she swore her nose tingled from the salt and pepper of his hair.

"I know you're worried, but you know how much I've been preparing for this. Don't you have any faith in me?" The words fell out of her mouth a bit sharper than she had intended, but she added no elaborations.

Jim's face remained unmoved like a victim of Medusa. It failed to reveal any emotion or worry that had crawled into his mind. His feet shifted, but he tried his best to remain calm. "What if you've forgotten to pack something? What if you lose your way or encounter some creature?" He considered allowing her to answer, but continued anyway. "What if you trip and dislocate your arm and you don't have the strength to return safely?"

Their eyes met. Her pupils bore into his, digging in and scooping out his insecurities and uncertainties, leaving them to dry in the rain. He considered apologizing, her eyes convincing him horribly, but no sound came out. The clock continued to tick, and she knew what his intentions really were. Her eyes dug deeper.

"Perhaps it's an instinct," he told Clara. "Perhaps there's a part of me that knows that if you leave, something will happen and I will never be able to see you again. Perhaps the universe is giving me this feeling for a reason, Clara."

Clara heaved a sigh, and all of her retaliation from her lungs. "Have you been taking your medications?"

"This has nothing to do with that," Jim scoffed, turning his head. He was now the one gawking at the clock, as though its ticking echoed and amplified with a glance. He felt his hands beginning to quiver as though the ticks of the clock were infecting him.

"I'm just saying you might be worrying over nothing," Clara justified.

"It's not worrying, Clara," he argued lightly. "It's called being a father."

"Fatherly instinct," she repeated back to him with the slightest taste of condescension. "The doctor said they come in waves, didn't he?"

"Clara, it's not that."

"And he instructed that when you start worrying about it that you need to ground yourself."

Jim sighed.

"Or would you like me to do it for you?" She took the silence to signify his approval. "I'm not Mother. I'm not searching for a way out, and I'm not going to disappear on you. You raised me yourself, and you know that I know better than that and that I see more worth in you than that. You mean so much to me, Father."

Jim's statued look was defeated by a small smirk. Clara understood her victory and smiled and nodded her head. "She would be so proud of you," he admitted. Only the clock responded this time. The tempo in his quivering hand skipped.

Jim helped Clara with her final check of her equipment, speaking only through blank facial expressions as a tribute to his taciturn defeat. Clara checked through her equipment thoroughly twice more and finally slipped her arms through the straps of her backpack. Her determination pressed on the front door, only to hesitate with Jim's offer to drive her to the airport himself and send her off. She imagined he would spit some stories of her youth and pluck memories that she had long forgotten (for better or for worse) with intentions she would have to interpret herself. But as the rusty pickup truck slowly crawled over the rocky path towards the border of the two worlds, they remained in utter silence as if the atmosphere held its frigid palms to their lips. With every bump that the rusty truck overcame, the two shook a little more, adding another drop in Jim's stomach and another spring in Clara's shoes. The imminent clouds grew closer, almost swelling as the truck approached its destination. It was as though their sunken eyes congregated like adolescents around a tragedy, pointing and laughing their own insecurities away at the expense of another. But they simply hovered overhead, their gazes enveloping and terraforming pits to Jim's stomach– a pit that might beckon his one and only daughter closer to the arms of Hades.

Finally, the truck hauled to a stop as he pulled up to the curb of the airport, the bumper not entirely in line. The air felt denser, as though the circulation of respiration was layering on top of all of the scenarios that loomed within Jim's mind. The airport is not a place to linger; it's full of busy people and never-ending queues that only induce anxiety and the slight impression of importance. Clara found herself glancing at her wrist once more as Jim shifted the gear into park.

Clara leapt down from the truck and pulled her pack over her shoulders. She began preparing a hasty goodbye for her father, only to realize he still sat in the car. She took two lengthy steps into the airport before she suddenly received a thick drop in her stomach. She decided to follow her intuition and turned back just in case. She figured nothing would go wrong on her journey into the mountains, but knew that her father would worry day and night, regardless. She hurried her way back to the truck, momentarily turning her head over her shoulder to keep a close eye on the time. She had to hurry her goodbye in order to check into her flight in time, but knew her guilt at this moment could not walk in her shoes.

She reached the truck and placed a reluctant hand on the window and the other on the handle of the vehicle. She pulled the door open and smiled at Jim.

"I'll be fine, Father," she comforted. Her words fell off her tongue onto his shoulder, but they slipped down his arm with the rhythm of a splatter of rain. "Father," she urged once more with the hopes of gaining his attention. His eyes broke the trance, and his gaze met his daughter's. In a brief second, he recalled every single moment of fear he felt when raising her. He imagined all of the times he cautiously and frantically raised his daughter without a wife beside him and saw every single instance in which the most insignificant mishaps pushed his little girl into the near grasp of death. The same shivers that possessed him in those moments found him now, and he knew that fear had him caged.

"Clara," his voice cracked. He cleared his throat and pushed all the doubt down his esophagus. "Do know that whether you stay or go, I will always worry about you. There will always be something new for me to fear. I only want what is best for you. Do know, Clara, that this fear comes not out of your incapabilities but simply of my own nightmares of being a father. I love you, Clara, and I wish you a safe and easy journey."

"Thank you, Father." She bit her lip to prevent her smile. She wrapped her arms around him and knew her journey could finally begin. All of the times she took over as the mother figure in the household would pay off in this moment. She would finally be able to disassociate herself from the image she had painted since she was twelve years old. This was the moment. She pulled away from the embrace, and Jim patted her shoulder. "Goodbye."

She adjusted her backpack as if she pulled the sun down with it and set off into the forests with her shoulders back and her spine straight. The spark of the setting sun obstructed her view of her father and turned his face into a fading silhouette. A cold breeze forced its way between them, rattling them, perhaps from the draft of an ascending plane. It was almost as though the sky was whispering her secrets. She turned away from her father and didn't look back. She finally released her smile.

Chapter Two

How unfortunate it is that this day has hung its hat on our rack so much sooner than expected.

"Doug, I'm not too sure about this anymore."

The weight of their joints creaked as the couple trekked through the woods, their backs hunched the slightest bit more from the weight of their backpacks, but their minds focused on aches much deeper than their spines. Personally, her hip was groaning and clicking like hands on a clock winding down to her retirement. She ached and tried to read his body language to determine whether he felt something similar, but all signals were ambiguous. The two stood unaware, however, of the overarching threats that lived within the pine, the seemingly innocent invisible eyes whose pupils mirrored their movements. Their foreign dialect barely differed from other visitors, as so few people came into the forest that all tongues appeared strange in their own way. These two, for instance, seemed completely clueless of the tales told of their setting.

"No, Macie, this is just fine. It'll be you and me and no one else for miles and miles. The locals even said that no one really comes here anyway." Doug placed a hand on his spouse's shoulder with many intentions, open to whatever she may interpret it as. She shook it off with disinterest.

"The local *children*," Macie emphasized. "Is it a bit much? I thought the tourist view was enough." She was waiting for a response but knew not to hold her breath. "What if there are bears? Do forests like these have bears? I read that this one species–"

"With the racket you're making, we'll be sure to scare 'em off," Doug retorted with aim to redirect the topics.

"They said no one's ever seen the ravine. What makes you think we're going to? I thought we were just going to stay a day or two at the treeline."

"They said *pretty much* no one's ever seen the ravine. Said that if you make it to see it, then you should feel grateful. At least that's what the translator said. Couldn't quite make out his accent. The point is that they know it exists, so that means people have seen it. It's gorgeous. We've only heard good things. That means we go looking for it, we find it, yay for us. What else do you want?" Macie lagged behind as Doug continued on. After a realization, he exhaled and turned around to face her. "What? What is it?"

"I just don't think it'll be enough, Doug." Her field of vision angled away from her husband in an attempt not to address her sorrows as what they were, but still allowed her face to contort itself to demonstrate her annoyance. She brushed a branch away from her head and released it, quickly. It made the arm of the tree to ricochet off its flexible structure and bounce back to whip her in the back. She pretended not to be bothered by the prickles it left on her shirt.

"Listen, I know what you saw looked bad, and it kind of was, but I swear it really wasn't! Just listen to me!" He reached for her shoulder again, this time grasping it and pulling her to face him. The two stopped, and he placed his right hand on her shoulder to match his left upon her other shoulder. His eyes stared into hers with sincerity, but hers appeared dull and dissatisfied. "There are no women out here. It's just you and me, Macie. Nothing to tempt me-" She rolled her eyes, shook off his hands, and turned away. "-

except you!" he offered, stepping in front of her in hopes of gaining her attention once again. "What was that thing Dr. Corzett said?" Macie continued her blank stare. "Something like, 'New experiences, newfound love?'"

Macie's eyes pierced through him, her contemplation apparent and slowly cracking through Doug's skin. In her mind, she hoped that her gaze would seep through those very cracks and cleanse their differences, but she knew that if she ventured into his body, she would see him formulating different responses within his skull to benefit him in whichever way he could. None of those responses within his mind would admit to his faults, but rather scrap together empty excuses. She would have to open him up more to get him to actually talk about it in order to get some legitimate forgiveness out of him, so she finally smiled. "Fine," she said in a stern voice. "We can camp for two nights, total. If you misbehave, I'm going to leave you here alone. We go by *my* rules. Do you hear me, Doug?"

He smiled and immediately came to life. "Yes, of course, my darling! Anything for you!" He went to place his hand on her shoulder once more, but was intercepted by her hand.

"Don't touch my shoulders like that," she commanded, and began to continue on through the trail.

"Hey! I married those shoulders!" he reminded her and tried to catch up with her quickened pace.

"You married the woman they're attached to!" She pretended not to see him, shrugging and focused forwards on the trail. She pressed her shoulders back, took a deep breath, and tried to understand whether what they followed was truly a trail at all or just space between pines. She felt at this moment as though the density of the trees was suffocating her, as she pictured them swelling beneath the bark until they would ultimately split open and spill their sappy contents over their clothes. It would be a nuisance to launder.

She peeked over after a few seconds to see him making no particular face. She took a deep breath and tried to figure out how to get him to feel sorry about anything at all. "Why *did* you marry me?" she questioned quietly.

"Hmm?" he responded, her words lost in the folds of his brain.

"Why did you marry me?" she reiterated. "It wasn't just my shoulders." She waited a few seconds. "It better not have been."

Doug took a few seconds to formulate what answer his spouse might be looking for. "You were so beautiful and I knew you had to be mine," he responded, not necessarily caring much for the cliche of his answer, or even the fact that he was audibly disinterested.

"I *was* beautiful?"

"Uh-huh," he said without thinking. He realized his mistake like he had been struck by lightning. "I mean, yeah, you were beautiful! But you're still beautiful! Just a different type of beautiful now!" he finessed.

"A different type?"

"Yeah."

"Like how Sheryl was a different type of beautiful?"

"What?"

"Answer me!" demanded Macie. She threw her voice into the horizon, the words scurrying away from her, never to be taken back. She lowered her voice in hopes of appearing to have more control of the situation, but really knew it was because she hated listening to people shout. "Please, Doug. Please answer."

"I mean yeah, kinda," he responded. "If you're really looking for an answer, then yes."

"Explain."

"What?"

"*Explain!*" Macie emphasized. She was not willing to listen to her husband for the next two days. She wanted to work through their issues and learn to enjoy time with him if only he would let it happen.

"Jeez, okay. Sheryll is just. . . a different type of beautiful. She's like. . ." He searched for the right words but could only think of one. "She's like hot, is all." Macie could hardly think of a response, so Doug continued. "Like she looks so much younger than she is- not saying she's too old, really. Or you. She just looks younger, maybe. You know? And I guess she's got a great body. Almost makes you feel guilty to think about it. I dunno."

There was too much to respond to. Macie struggled in considering what to focus on first, but was thrown off most of all by his word choice of "guilty." Macie could live with being considered old, she could live with not being beautiful anymore, but she couldn't even think to live with the weight of knowing that the only thing to make Doug feel even *slightly* guilty was how he felt about his sister-in-law's body. "Tell me again how it happened," she demanded before she could even process the words coming out of her mouth. She spat them up like bile- something toxic inside of her that had been rotting for much too long, that drove her further into illness as she held on. But the words were out now, hanging in the air, waiting for someone to react to them.

Something shattered within Doug- hot and sharp. The fragments penetrated into his skin, and his anger seeped out of the deepened cuts. He refused to consider the consequences of his words. "Listen, Macie, I'm *really* sorry that you're taking this so personally."

"Because it *is* personal!" she shrieked.

"Lower your voice!"

"We're *alone,* Doug! Are you *that* ashamed to be around me?" Her voice filled the air, and when the echoes finally laid themselves in the distance, the silence that grew from its seeds only continued to swell and crawl. It suffocated Doug, and the shards of his patience struggled to defend him.

"It just. . . happened."

"No! No more of that!" Macie cried, furious at his state of emotion rather than her own. The chaos in her mind would rest when she could finally tear the proper reaction from Doug's throat. "You're going to give me everything! Every detail! Anything you can possibly give because you gave it all to *her*!"

"Gave *what* to her?" he growled in return. "It was nothing! It didn't mean anything, she didn't mean anything, but you're blowing it up like you always do!" They continued walking, neither side willing to give up. Their stubbornness welcomed the silence. Occasionally, the silence was accompanied by some harsh mutters under Macie's breath, but otherwise their taciturn journey traveled between them, an arm around their shoulders appearing both hostile and utopian. However, their stubbornness was not simply in the name of their argument but rather their own ideals reflecting how they believed their marriage could be pieced together. They needed this time only to scurry upon the floor to find the shards that left their bloodied hands so hungry for a miracle. And so, it came.

"Is this a stream?" Macie questioned aloud, not necessarily expecting an answer. She received one anyway.

"It is." Doug's voice carried a hint of interest and a hint of hope that the water would be an emblem of something even greater. "We should find level ground so we can set up camp nearby."

"Why can't we keep going?" she asked despite her aching joints. Perhaps sharing the twinge would be the last nail in the coffin.

She fantasized about Doug- not like he ever fantasized about her, though. She would picture the two of them back in their prime and how he would have done anything to keep her by his side. But those days were over, and things had changed immensely. She imagined the two of them meeting the ravine and seeing it for all of its glory, and then Doug would turn to her and look her in the eyes as though it was the first time they ever met. This would heal their marriage, yes, and she was determined to ensure it would happen.

"Listen," he interrupted, his raspy voice disrupting her fantasy. "We found a stream, and it's important to stick to it. We can rest now and then continue in the morning. We ain't in any rush, so don't bother rushing. You're just gonna hurt yourself. Or me." Her cheeks pinkened as he spoke her mind. She pretended as though he hadn't been correct, but eventually came to the conclusion that the only person she would be convincing was herself. So, she let it be. Doug turned away from her and shuffled away. With only a few steps, he was already disappearing into the pines, each tree like a body in a crowd, obscuring her view of him. "I'll look in this direction and you'll go… anywhere but this direction."

Macie nodded, hardly caring that Doug once again took over the situation and refused to allow her to make decisions. She blamed herself for being the one to have pointed out the stream, but was glad to have found it in the first place. With the sun now peaking in the sky, trickles of sweat had started to run down her neck and trapped underneath her shirt, humidity forming. She glanced upwards as though greeting the sun would lessen her burden, but was only met with the lattice of light through the leaves as though heat was trying its best to break through the fingers of the branches. Komorebi (noun)– the sunlight breaking and filtering through the leaves.

It was as though she was staring up at the throat of the forest, and it was preparing to contract its esophagus and swallow her whole. The added weight to her back hardly helped, and she knew that the source of water would serve them immense aid. She took a few moments to travel to the stream and dip her hands in the thin water, and was disappointed to find that the refreshing frigidness she had been expecting had failed her, but rather singed her fingertips. Looking closely, she noticed that steam seemed to be rising from the water as if it was boiling and evaporating before her. It began to form a thick mist like a swarm of wasps, the humidity soaking into her scalp and raising some loose hairs. It swirled and danced around with the coagulating fog as though an inaudible song was playing a tune she would never recognize.

She took a few steps away from the diminishing stream, then turned and sought to catch up with her husband. Something was not right. Between the evaporating water and evaporating spouse, Macie knew that two days on this mountain would surely be plenty. She knew that despite her arguments with Doug, it was imperative that she inform him of what was happening. This was not safe.

She thought running might be more effective, but with her coming of age, she didn't think she would last very long. She thought about how, when she got back home, she would start taking runs in the morning to boost her stamina and increase the health of her heart. And so to start her on her journey, she would jog lightly for a few seconds and then slow back to a walk, only to repeat the process. She figured she would be able to locate the stream again if she tried, and even concluded that it would be useless to them in a matter of moments, completely sucked into the air through a straw of mist. It was no longer of importance to them. And so, she pulled away from the stream and called out for her husband.

"Doug?" she cried, slightly out of breath. "Doug, where are you?" She continued, slowing down as she got further into the forest, the trees thickening. The roots beneath her feet almost seemed to grab at her ankle, each outrageous shape and bump demonstrating their old age.

The roots appeared almost like the brains of the forest, exposed and vulnerable, yet they paved the way for the growth of the trees and the branches that came as a result. One might describe them similarly to the gyri and sulci of the brain. Just as vulnerable, the forest floor held secrets and information. They told the tales of all others who crossed through these paths. What had happened to them? What was so devastating about these woods? What kept the locals from lobotomizing the trees and decapitating the roots, perhaps building over them to create something of more use to society?

"Doug?" Macie continued to cry. How long had she been running? It felt like it had been at least thirty minutes. *What a dumb idea,* she thought to herself, forever criticizing her husband. *How were we supposed to regain contact with each other?* She nearly tripped over a root. *No form of communication. Not a second thought to it.* She slowed down to catch her breath. She decided to take a different approach and listen instead. It was almost as though the heart of the forest was beating. She heard sounds, but none of them could be distinguished as human. There was the faint white noise of rushing water, most likely from the stream, but that was it.

And then the fear hit her like a poison that had been creeping through her veins, awaiting the perfect moment to grip around her throat. She gasped for air. *He did this on purpose,* convinced a voice in the back of her mind. The heartbeat became louder. Her throat constricted more. *He did this to get rid of me.* The tightness in her throat made it ache to swallow.

"Doug?" she shouted, yielding no results. Not an echo returned to her, but rather the crescendoing beating of a heart. She choked. "Doug, please!" It beat harder. "Doug!"

Something sounded from behind her. Her immediate thought was of her husband. Logic determined he would not have been able to appear behind her. Logic was not on her mind. She fought for it. Was she turned around? Impossible. In which direction had he headed? She must have found herself turned around. The forest was incredibly thick, after all. It must be incredibly easy to lose oneself.

She turned. "Doug?"

And the last thing she heard was that very same venom of fear contracting within her arteries that swelled like tumors overtaking her flesh. So, she shrieked as though it were the antidote.

Chapter Three

I had hoped the beckoning fingers of death would have taken my hand before yours, but unfortunately, we cannot control the body to which it belongs.

The moon glared as though the sky were its hostage. The usual grimacing snow scurried down from the heavens like bombs. The ground, previously singed by the unbearable beams of the sun, welcomed this nightly winter as it gathered crystallized flakes in its arms. This growing dandruff of the sky collected on the ground like sand crumbling into the hourglass, yet somehow ticked its warnings for the conclusion of the night. She found a slightly elevated clearing with potential and immediately set her backpack down in order to start creating her shelter. As she worked, she began to think of her worrying father and wondered how he would feel seeing her in this moment. Clara knew that no matter what situation she would be in, Jim would worry about her, but she chose to imagine how proud he would be when she returned.

She shook the thoughts away, along with some determined snow that had accrued in a few strands of loose hair. Snow was most expected, but the same could not be said about the troubles in her mind. Thoughts came back with an orangey taste of nostalgia and uprooted memories that had diminished as time departed them. The snow was different, though. She could prepare for the snow and the frigid temperature that accompanied it. She could prepare for the hiking the freezing, and scorching. But she could not prepare for the memories. Ill-equipped and tired of their stupefaction, she allowed them to flow back.

Clara pictured warm, outstretched arms of an entity compassionate to her, the flashback carrying youth back into her body. She could remember gazing into these deep brown eyes as though they were a picture slathered on the lining of her skull. Cradled in her arms, she would look up and see the coils of her hair, and think to herself about how much she hoped to replicate the styled curls one day. Something about it was comforting and, in a sense, refreshing. Should she come back from kindergarten battered because David Paterson made fun of her for being "dirt colored," she would return home to her mother's arms and see where beauty truly lies. Warm hugs and soft kisses would bandage the wounds around her skin and ensure her that it would all disappear, blown over by the prickling sands that cover it.

She was much too young to remember the days when she grew from spitting bubbles to babbles and swaddling to toddling. No matter where her adventurous young soul brought her, her mother was always there to care for her. She had originally been reluctant to go and leave the safe arms of her mother in order to begin her days at grade school, but with a kiss to the forehead and a rub of the arm, she was convinced. After all, mother does know best. She knew that whatever would come her way would easily be handled, for by the end of the day, she would be back in sight of her mother's warm eyes.

She did, however, remember one memory in particular when she had caught a stomach bug as a child and had to stay home with her mother. She had grown accustomed to school and, as she refused to admit, was a little nervous about leaving the routine she had fallen into. She could not articulate it, but consistency offered her a comfort she could not replicate. Spending time with her mother brought back the slightest pieces of memories she had and how pleasant they had been. Her mother held her in her arms without minding the illness that riddled her body, and gently swayed back and forth. She smelled of citrus, perhaps oranges, and her voice was light and melodious like the familiarity of a song that rocked her in the womb. She could only assume by this that the quavering tunes and gentle embrace had healed her. It was these moments that she held onto, her mother's coiled black hair forming a veil over the two of their faces, and that sweet orange tang intoxicating her and reminding her that this moment was beyond dreams and suppressant of nightmares.

But it was those coiled curls and notes of orange that she would miss the most when her mother started disappearing. Perhaps it was that her youth altered the way time was perceived. It made ten minutes seem like an entire day, but somehow an entire season crumbled into a week. It certainly paid no assistance that her mother would never disappear for the same amount of time, anywhere between days and months. It was a mystery that she never could comprehend, especially considering how her earliest years with her mother were all spent within the confines of their house. She would spend countless hours sitting on her knees on the sofa, her hands impatiently pressed on the top cushions. She watched the cars go by, and wondered when her mother would return. The fact that she did, indeed, have the youthful, timeless mind bothered her naught, but rather burned in her mind the same image of the street and the occasional neighbor tending to their front garden. It never dawned on her how strange it was that the family only had one car, still in Jim's possession. Young girls never thought of such technicalities.

Somewhere along the way, there had been a shift. Jim was starting to occupy the office that he had rarely used prior to these disappearances. He had usually gone to work during the day in order to provide for the family. It happened so subtly that Clara never realized that a change was whirling around her until the thought struck her like an electrostatic shock from a touch on a winter day. Her mother was home less, and her father was home more. It was like an hourglass she hoped would never run out.

The sand was just beginning to cover the bottom of the hourglass. It became more common for Jim to sit at his desk in the office at home. Some boxes had accumulated, dusty from some spring cleaning or another, years ago. They would be moved in time, but for now, the space would have to account for the hours he was picking up. He requested that Clara spend her time in the office with him so that he would be able to watch over her better, but unfortunately, there was never anything of entertainment to her in this room. The walls were an obsolete yellow, and the floors were a dusty hardwood. The toys her family owned, she had long grown out of, and she was much too shy to make friends at school, as she felt it difficult to relate to the other children and found she had little to say. Whenever she would express her boredom to Jim, he would respond that she could work on her school work or read a book. To Clara's dismay, because her father was working so often and her mother was absent, there was never time for anyone to take her out to buy new books, and so she read the recycled stories until she was numb to the emotions they were hoping to convey.

"Dad?" Her voice barely reached the drum. He continued to work away as though there was a wall between them. "Dad?" she asserted after a slight pause. He held up one finger as if to demonstrate the number of eternities she would have to wait for his response. "Dad, where's Mom?" It was a question she hadn't quite anticipated would leave her mouth. Surely, it was one she often thought of, but she had never constructed her nerves to actually voice it. Fortunately for Clara, this question seemed to be the password.

He stopped working, and the gentle scribbling of pencil on paper came to a halt. He did not, however, turn his head. The world took a breath. "She's not present." The scribbling continued, although hesitant.

"What's she doing?" The next grain of sand collided-another halt. Although they were being produced at the rate of a typical conversation, it was as though she had opened up a box that was bustling with inquiries, only waiting for the day someone would set them free. And set them free, she did. They all came flooding out, and she could barely feel herself applying enough pressure to the wound to make the situation manageable enough. Pandora would be amazed.

The dust particles drifting in the room seemed to freeze in the air, struck by the overwhelming questions. They all turned to sand and contributed to the hurried piling in the hourglass. It took Jim longer to respond this time. He seemed to be debating whether he should turn away from his work or not. Knowing the importance of occupation, or perhaps the depth of the conversation, he refused to turn. "She's… an adventurer," he responded, partially unconfident, partially content. "She explores. She'll return, I imagine." The scribbling resumed; this time, seemingly convinced that it blocked any further questions. It was clearly mistaken.

"When is she coming back?" Her question refused to hesitate.

Jim understood in this moment that with childhood came curiosity and that ignoring it would only amplify the situation. And so, he finally turned around to face his daughter. "I'm uncertain, Clara. Your mother," he thought long and hard about what to say next. How does one properly inform a child to ensure that the topics are appropriately explained? "Your mother is a difficult woman to comprehend at times. I can never quite understand her justifications, but I assure you that eventually, she will return to us."

Jim felt a conflict rising in his stomach. Although his vocabulary and manner of speech when interacting with his daughter were above her age level to demonstrate everything that he wanted his daughter to become, there were some topics that were too mature for her. Children are so often compared to sponges with their impeccable ability to absorb the waves of information they are introduced to on a daily basis. Especially considering how much time Clara spent with him at home, Jim wanted to ensure that she received the most soaking she would be able to retrieve in the given environment, albeit a controlled one.

With the answers to her questions only half resolved, like an unsatisfying last chord in a symphony, Clara decided it was time to go outside and spend some time on her own. While they didn't have the most entertaining backyard for a young girl, she still made use of the small space and her vast imagination. She pictured herself gaining the courage to ask to walk to the nearest park so she could use the swing set, and she imagined how much she would love the rocking motion, the chains of the swing clanging against the metal bars to which it held. Her coils would sway alongside her almost as though her mother was there with her, gently pressing her onwards to the trees and back again. But Clara's confidence had run out, and Jim's responses only tired her further. She instead drew in the ground with twigs and pulled up blades of grass, some by the root and some by the blade. They each made different sounds, and she plucked away from them as if to compose a symphony of her own. She loves me. She loves me not. A childish game was never meant to be played with a mother figure in mind.

And then she met Jessica Heathers. The hourglass was a third full by then. Clara was quite a bit older when the two of them finally introduced themselves. She wasn't quite sure what type of friend she would wind up with, but she never pictured it would be someone such as Jessica Heathers. They were in high school, somewhere around 15 or 16 years old-they couldn't quite remember. They were seated next to each other in a social studies class in which the teacher was rather strict, especially with his assigned seating arrangement. He announced that they were to be paired together for the majority of the school year and that they were to become acquainted with those seated beside them. During testing, of course, the rows of desks would be rearranged to better prevent cheating, although this would never stop the average deviant.

Jessica Heathers was the type of girl whom you would refer to by her first and surname, although no one could really pinpoint why. Perhaps it was that there was another young girl named Jessica in their grade, although they were never in the same place together, and it helped to discern during gossiping. Strangely, those who knew nothing of this second Jessica (whose surname was Williams) still referred to Jessica Heathers as such. Perhaps the other students simply preferred the way "Jessica Heathers" rolled off the tongue, almost as if her parents had put careful thought and planning into her name. Or perhaps, it was simply that her name fit so well with her personality, as though she woke up every morning and applied each letter like a layer of blush, the pigment perfectly complimenting her skin tone.

She had relatively pale skin, although you imagine it should pinken with the embarrassed blush, should it ever glow through her foundation, and ignore the sense of confidence she carried that would never allow her any sense of embarrassment at all. She was the type of girl you never expected would have had any imperfections of the skin, though one could never predict, considering the powder setting her first layer carefully slathered on, taking at least half an hour of gazing into her careful reflection. She lightly lined her eyes and darkened her lashes as if to frame the beauty of her eyes, both in shape and color. While other girls like Darla Quincy would constantly brag about the hue of her iris, Jessica Heathers would remain humble to the point where you would only notice the emerald green in the middle of the conversation when you finally build up the confidence to look her in the eyes as if for the first time.

But for Clara, it only took her the first time. When the teacher instructed them to introduce themselves, she was immediately teleported to a land where the green of Jessica Heathers' eyes lined the terrain and the bluest skies hung over the land. She saw the clouds like bread dough in the sky, the wind kneaded them leisurely, occasionally twirling and intertwining with the branches of trees. And there was music. Could it have been violins? A soft French horn, perhaps? Something delicate yet versatile tangled its soundwaves in the fingers of grass as though the entirety of the fields below were trembling with the sincerity of the tune. The music stopped.

Clara realized that the very music gracing her ears had been the voice of Jessica Heathers introducing herself. She was not able to deduce her introduction, as she was distracted by her grace, and so her response could only have been an embarrassing, "Huh?"

She laughed, and the music filled her ears again. "I said I'm Jessica Heathers," she reiterated with a genuine kindness.

"I'm Clara Brown," she responded with her arm outstretched, anxiously awaiting the moment their hands would clasp together, joining their bodies. Her hands were delicate and soft, but her handshake was confident and somehow sent an optimistic vibration, as though through this handshake, she knew that the two of them would become great friends.

"Is it just me, Clara?" Jessica Heathers began, leaning in a little bit. "Or is Mr. Khan a little…?" She made a gesture to indicate the absurdity of the teacher's strict introductions.

Clara laughed. "Absolutely."

"By the way, your hair is so gorgeous," Jessica Heathers complimented. "The curls, the color- just beautiful!"

Heat flooded into Clara's cheeks. "Thank you," she responded, trying to build up the courage to redirect the remark.

"I wish I had hair more like yours," Jessica Heathers continued. "I love how your hair color flatters your skin tone. Do you tan?"

"No."

"Oh, then do you dye your hair?"

"No." She smirked and avoided getting lost in her eyes again.

"So, you're just naturally this beautiful? Absolutely amazing. I love it!"

Clara continued to smile, and the heat dissipated from her cheeks to her ears. She pictured the way her father appeared when he tended to blush, but knew that she was safe with her darker complexion. "You're beautiful, too," she expressed. "And I love your hair too. I bet everyone tells you that all the time, though."

"Aw, you're sweet," she started. "But I'm sure you must get it more often than me."

"Actually," she began thinking about all those who would comment on her look. As beautiful as Jessica Heathers was, she wasn't quite sure how much she could be trusted with the burden of the stories of these bullies. She decided to dilute her story. "I don't really talk to too many people," she punctuated.

"That's a shame," Jessica Heathers divulged. "You'll have to come hang out with me and my boyfriend sometime."

My boyfriend. The word struck through Clara's heart, and she could have sworn she felt it deflating. She felt the corners of her lips drag down, and her smile disappeared. She didn't want to make her feelings obvious, especially not to this girl she hardly knew. And of course, she *certainly* did not want to meet this boyfriend.

***

The hourglass was half full. Jessica Heathers and her boyfriend didn't last. They broke up, and the two girls walked in the woods together while Jessica Heathers listed everything he had done wrong in their relationship and how vulnerable she felt to let it happen. She expressed how absolutely foolish she must have been to let a man such as this into her life and control her decisions and ideas the way he did.

"And would you believe that he said I *owed* it to him?" Jessica Heathers concluded her story. She pulled her sleeve past her wrist even though the sun beamed through the branches.

"That's ridiculous!" Clara responded, and turned her head from the trail to look her friend's lamenting eyes. "You do so much for him. You owe him nothing."

"But he kept insisting and *insisting* and I just..."

Clara nodded intensely, completely enveloped by the drama of the story as well as her friend's well-being.

"I threw my soda at him and left!"

"As he deserves!"

"And I walked home!"

"Did he come after you?"

"Of course, he didn't!"

Clara felt her nose scrunch, a kind of rage demonstrated in her face that she could never convey with her words. And so instead, she said this:

"You know you deserve better than that, right, Jessica Heathers?" Her friend wiped away a stray tear. "You are so strong-so much stronger than you realize. And you're smart too. You know what you deserve, and you're not afraid to allow yourself the environment you need in order to ensure your happiness. I know it seems really difficult, but I assure you that the way you responded- that's the strength within you. That's the Jessica Heathers who deserves someone who will treat her right."

"You think so?" she sniffed.

Clara nodded. "And if anyone ever treats you like this again? They'll have to deal with me." They paused their walk. "I promise you that I will not allow anyone to ever make you feel this way ever again. And if I break that promise, you'll still have my shoulder if you ever need it."

Unfortunately, promises were broken, and this became a common occurrence between the two. It seemed as though Jessica Heathers had a different boyfriend every week. This most likely wasn't true, as Clara's memory must have been exaggerated to some degree, but it left her with a heartache each time and only made her more determined to have the beautiful Jessica Heathers reciprocate the same friendship Clara expressed to her. Some days she would speak so rapidly that Clara could only nod intensely at the stories being told, other days they would simply lie in the grass, perhaps shaded under a tree or in a meadow, while Jessica Heathers dejected monotonously about how she feared she would never find true love, although tears would never stain the painted bags of her eyes. As the seasons progressed, her long sleeves became less conspicuous.

Clara was always distrusting of these boys as they arrived in Jessica Heathers' life. One would be too arrogant, and another rather unintelligent. Perhaps one would be deemed too offensive, or one would smell a little too sour, or would have a nasally voice that quivered in her ears uncomfortably. There was always something that led Clara to believe that Jessica Heathers deserved someone much better than him. Still yet, she would never fail to rant to Clara about the imperfections of her relationships, perhaps a bit too late for them to be fixed, only for them to crumble apart like a fragile leaf.

***

Clara now sat inside her tent, watching the falling snow scurry through the air, reflections of the molecules released from her breath in the form of clouds. She thought to herself about these times and all of the regrets that she held. It was always a different hike she and Jessica Heathers would continue on as she listened to her friend complain about those who had wronged her. She imagined each snowflake held its own moment in time and felt the weight of them as they bundled up at the roots of trees, some of them dissolving, but the preponderance of them clinging to each other as if to string together the different illustrations. Pictures upon pictures floated down from the heavens, each one taking a second to breathe as it touched Clara's body, then slowly dissolving. Would she hold onto them and allow the heat of her body to overwhelm the crystal of their molecules, or simply allow them to continue on their own accounts and affect her in whichever way they could? Whatever she would decide, she pulled up her scarf, feeling the gathered moisture from her breath dampen her nose. She imagined Jessica Heathers was beside her at this time, her sleeves pulled into her palms as though to substitute mittens, but the air was much too frigid for her to picture the heat of her body against her own.

What Magic Lurks in the Mountains?

By Seymour Duffelburg

There are many myths, conspiracies, and curiosities associated with the mountains, as it has been a relatively prominent location for odd activity throughout the centuries. We examine them and come to consider what we could possibly learn about this mysterious site within nature, and perhaps delve deeper into our research so we are able to answer the questions that humanity has been asking throughout time.

The oldest tale we were able to trace back refers to the widowed soul of Jane Prodigia. Jane Prodigia had married young due to an unexpected pregnancy and was forced to raise her daughter alone due to her husband's draft in the ongoing war. Unfortunately, she received a message describing the death of her husband (which is believed to be an impalement), which resulted in her dedicating her life to searching for his soul. She was stricken with skepticism, and part of her was drawn to the mountains. It came to her in a dream that each tree within the forest would house a single soul, and in her mind, she thought that seeking out her deceased husband's soul would yield her peace of mind and the ability to understand his death. "[Jane] searched with a fire that could warm a room, but failed to open the chimney, which resulted in a billowing plume of smoke to obscure her perspectives," writes author Pendleton Siggs to depict the deep desire but near-insanity of her pursuit.

There is some documentation that has either been lost, burned, thrown into a river, or simply never existed that comes from a close friend, family member, or neighbor that states that Jane's dream depicted crimson lights pulsating within the trunks of the trees like hearts, with the exception of one which beat yellow. It caused her to believe that it was not just the soul of her husband, but the soul of her soulmate.

And so, with that, Jane Prodigia set off into the mountains to familiarize herself with each of the infinitude of trees so she could find the yellow glow and pledge her goodbyes. She never returned, and the locals rumored that her own soul now resides within the forest, the innocence of her ambitions now resonated within the trunk of the largest tree.

Another myth that is associated with the mountains originated from a flower that was expected to cause one to fall in love when its dried petals were boiled down into a tea. In this particular myth a young musician (the instrument of his choice varies between tales but the most common interpretations include the pan flute, lyre, hurdy gurdy) by the name of Gerard Wittergan, set off on a journey to find the flower so he could elope with his projected lover, a lover who was arranged to marry a less-than-favorable man with plenty of wealth. The legend claims that Gerard set off to hike into the mountains to find this flower, which has never been seen by human eyes. There are plenty of guesses as to which flower this might have been, but considering the environment of the mountains themselves, it is highly unlikely that flowers would have been able to blossom there during the time of this myth, let alone now. This didn't hinder Gerard's journey, however. He set off into the mountains, convinced that he would find the flowers blossoming within the ravine (although it is not noted in any of the myths what drove him to this conclusion), with the belief that he would one day return and be able to capture the heart of his beloved. While Gerard never reappeared, some claim that they hear music coming from the treeline on nights when the wind is still. Some believe he is singing his goodbyes or vows, or confessions to his love, but the words are masked through the trees. Only the timbre of a heartbroken voice is able to ooze through.

Other tales trace back to the Heedsboro Hysteria incident in which approximately 850 citizens of a nearby town were stricken with the impulse to peel skin away from their forearms. The incident resulted in the hospitalization of nearly 400 citizens. Best-case scenarios yielded splotches of scarring, and worst-case scenarios resulted in three known deaths. It was said that should the infected civilians dip their forearms in the river of the mountains, they would be healed of their ailments, and so began a migration of hysterical humans haunting the forests in search of the river. Further information in regards to their return is undocumented which causes historians to wonder if any retreated at all.

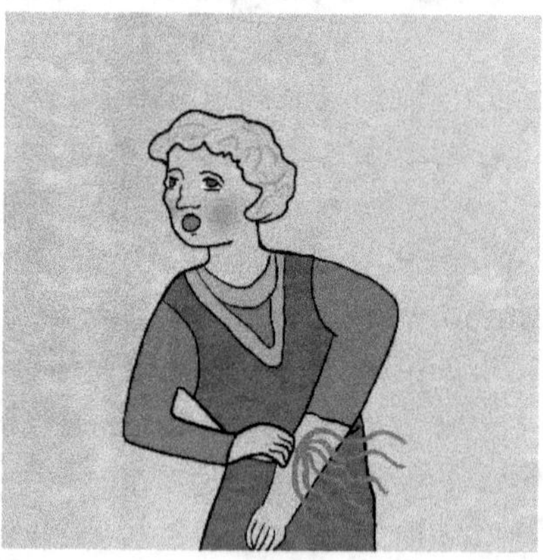

The Heedsboro Hysteria had an impact on the local churches, who believed that the Hysteria was a result of demons possessing sinners (most commonly for anxiety, refusing confession, or witchcraft). Because of this and the highly religious beliefs of Heedsboro, many of the infected were shunned by their families, given exorcisms, or, in eleven cases, failed crucifixions. The general consensus of the healthy was that the demons were scouting out a location for the throne of the Devil himself. It was believed that the urge to dip the forearms into the river was an attempt to sacrifice the blood of the impure to allow for a foundation of this structure. From then on, those of religious beliefs who resided in Heedsboro would fail to associate with the mountains by all means necessary.

However, not all were driven away from the mountains as a result of this Hysteria. Some who failed to see logic within the religious beliefs began to wonder what other forces could have contributed to the strange number of disappearances correlated to the mountains. Conspiracy theorists and some paranoid biologists have implied there is evidence of sasquatches residing within the mountains. The size of these sasquatches is thoroughly debated throughout the community, some claiming that the puddles throughout the terrain are caused by the footprints and others believing that it is a single large sasquatch whose belly forms the height of the mountain itself. It may be assumed that after the disappointment of discovering that BigFoot was unfortunately an alien rather than a sasquatch, the belief in sasquatches would diminish when in reality it appeared to shift to the conspiracy hotspot of the mountains.

Some claimed that sasquatches would not be suitable for the environment in the mountains. The harsh snowstorms that beset the forests began to lead theorists to believe that, rather than sasquatches were yetis. They were able to continue to fit into the descriptions of the mountains so far while also maintaining the adaptability to the violent weather changes. But with this came the debate of how the yetis would continue to survive during the day, during which temperatures would climb and therefore prove hostile to their coats of thick fur.

One theorist in particular named Jeremiah Woodson, chose to reject both of these possibilities and instead wrote his thesis entitled "The dichotomy of sasquatch and yeti shattered: the chupacabra reins principle", which promptly determined the creature lurking to be the chupacabra. Considering how the name "chupacabra" translates to "goat-sucker", this clearly was met with plenty of backlash, and there is no confirmed life within these woods. Woodson clapped back at his naysayers by establishing that these particular chupacabra were raised cannibalistically and, therefore, only have to rely on themselves (and very careful mating and meal planning) for survival.

All myths, beliefs, and conspiracies aside, it is also important for us to note that it is also entirely possible that both, or none of these, could prove true. Unfortunately, we have not reached a point in technological advances that allows for safe travel within the mountains, but perhaps someday in the near future will come a time in which we will be able to uncover the truths behind the mysteries of the mountains.

Chapter Four

Although our time together has been limited, I can assure you, my darling, that my love for you is not.

To be young is to be ambitious, and to be both often means to be reckless. And with that imbues dreams of staying out beyond curfew and cause mischief across neighborhoods in which we would never ever see ourselves living until our early forties, when we finally have secured that position we've been longing for. Or perhaps one hides oneself away after a dispute with our mothers over the outfit we spent so much time stitching together for the events of the afternoon. After all, once youth is burned, the ashes cannot be rewound. It is so easily overlooked with our constant experiences, resulting in our necessary "next time, next time" mindset that we fail to truly enjoy it while it dances on our fingertips. And with that, Ethan, Johnson, and Shauna are introduced.

Johnson, a young man of the same age as the other two, lived solely on his insecurities, hiding away the parts of himself he hoped no one would ever see. Whether body or mind, he made do by wrapping, clothing, snipping, and suppressing. Should he ever find a fault in himself, he lay on the floor pushing out sit-ups and crunches until his body ached and caused him to question why he would ever do so much yet again. In the end, who was he *really* trying to impress? Himself? Others? He would never allow anyone else to see the body he had unwittingly achieved. He would never want anyone else to see the bumps and curves he tried so hard to hide away. And yet, there he was in a body that someone else would be so grateful to have, only to find that he was the very person looking for another body. Despite the hard exterior he felt he had, he was still rather slim and of a below-average height, and he knew that should he ever find himself in a quarrel, he would not have the heart to throw any punches but instead curl into a fetal position and abide.

He was never the type to fit in, as cliche as it may be. His parents came from different races, painting an ambiguous face and existential inquiry. He never truly discovered if he liked boys or girls or neither or both, and so he settled on the very same uncertainty that rested on his face. Every aspect of his life was dictated by this constant ambiguity of who (or even *what*) he was, even resulting in the use of his surname to glaze over the fact that he holds a blank opinion of his forename. Some days, he even allowed this billowing uncertainty to boil over, resulting in the questioning of "what do I look like?" or "is this a universal experience?" to people regardless of their relationship to him, and no matter the response, he was never satisfied. After all, a satisfied life has no risks in the moment.

Shauna Rivera, on the other hand, enjoyed the constant ups and downs of her life. She was not the typical troublemaker, for she still feared the iron fist of authority, but she took the time in her life to decide what her fate would be. And decide, did she, as she dove into as much adventure as a teenager could, taking anything she could into her hands and twirling it into something much shinier than the original. She was never sure where life would take her next, but rather allowed the world to direct her in whichever direction the universe seemed to find most fitting. Shauna had the curse of being a middle child, somewhat overlooked by her parents but still warranting some sort of responsibility. Her older sister, Isabella, was never the best role model for her, but rather demonstrated everything you shouldn't do, while her younger brother, Martin, was too young to form his own opinions and often sided with whatever option would provide him the best outcome. Her parents divorced soon after her brother's birth, confusing, but not entirely surprising Shauna and her sister.

Shauna was very much not like her sister, for she had a vast library of ambitions before her. Still rather young, in her eleventh year, she had much time to decide what path she would follow in life, whether the subject dictated science or literature, or art. She knew that her future required further studying to achieve all of the things her sister never would. As polar opposites, Shauna hoped that her ambitions would be enough to make up for the lack of motivation of Isabella, while also exemplifying to her kid brother the decisions one *should* make. She almost served as a second mother to her brother, Martin, as their father split from the scene the second he freed himself from his marriage. Isabella had told Shauna that one day she would find their father and live with him instead of her mother (with whom Isabella often quarreled), and discover her true family. While Shauna understood her sister's intentions, she knew that her heart belonged with her mother, and should she ever travel in life, it would not be very far from home.

And then, of course, there's Ethan, the boy with the jade green eyes, who had found himself overrun by trouble. He inserted himself into the duo (previously a trio until Angus Briar left) as the newest member. Something about Shauna and Johnson just struck the right note with him, and he decided that he would slither his way in. Although he didn't appear to enjoy their company, often pinching his wrist at some of their conversations, he still stayed put regardless. There's not much to be said about Ethan, at least not for now, as he chose to remain reticent in regards to matters in his life.

Taciturn (adjective)– feeling inclined to silence as if to hold one's own finger against his lips.

On this particular day, the trio found themselves hiking into the forest, infused with countless rumors and stories that were exhibited to them while on a school field trip, with the intention to learn the history behind a nearby town. Something about the threat of danger appears to humans of their age as a challenge or even perhaps a joke. Exploring dangerous, and even possibly haunted, forests would be much more exciting than their school field trip, at least. After all, what's the point of bringing a class to camp at a park near treacherous woods and discussing the known history of said woods if the students aren't allowed to explore it for themselves?

"Is this really a good idea?" Shauna asked the two, but more so Ethan. It had been his idea to ditch, after all. "What if there are bears?"

"There aren't going to be any bears. Besides, I've got the flare gun," Ethan responded, sticking a thumb backwards to gesture towards his backpack.

"What do you have a flare gun for?" Johnson asked.

"One of the teachers left me in charge of it. She said in case of emergency, and I know we're going to need it more than them back there."

"But what if-"

"I'm sure we're safe," Johnson reassured. "If they didn't want us wandering off into the woods, they wouldn't have brought us here. They know that people can't help but get curious. They didn't even fence off the woods or anything to keep us out. And I trust Ethan. I'm sure he wouldn't do anything to put us in danger, right, Ethan?"

Ethan saluted with two fingers pointed his forehead and then curling a sore wrist to swivel his fingers.

Shauna decided she would agree with the two of them, but couldn't help but tuck caution into the back of her mind. She continued to trek through the line of trees with the two boys, unable to shake the feeling in her core. It was as though the break in the trees held eyes, the light breaking between them imitating the reflective pupils of a patient predator, and while logically, she understood that this was light breaking through the branches, a pit grew in her stomach and blossomed whenever they would make eye contact. Regardless, she knew that no matter how much she protested, they would march on. She found herself walking through conversations in her head of how she would justify her behavior, should she and her comrades be reprimanded after their absence was detected. What excuse could she possibly give? Would punishment tamper with her chances of a better future? She focused on a more optimistic aversion.

"Have you guys started thinking about college yet?" Shauna asked as they invaded the treeline.

"A little," Johnson started. "I was thinking Community."

"Community? Really?" Shauna confirmed. "I could've sworn you were talking about Spinam."

He shrugged. "Plans change."

"I thought you would've been a good fit."

He shrugged once more. "Plans still change. Besides, they really don't have much prestige over other schools. If I'm gonna spend that much money, might as well be worth it, you know?"

Shauna nodded and waited for time to pass before her next question. "Have you decided on a major yet?" Part of her asked and she hoped that the question would be reflected unto her.

He shook his head. "I keep thinking that it's going to come to me one day, and it's going to be this big epiphany, and my life is going to fall into place. If I'm being realistic, I know that's probably not going to happen. Maybe I'll take some gen-eds and they'll give me a better idea of the direction I wanna go in, but right now I'm just staying undecided." He turned to face her. "What about you?"

She smiled. "Well, I'm caught between-"

"Oh my *God*," Ethan moaned. "If we wanted to hear about school and all that, we could've stayed behind. You know, with the school."

Silence followed.

"I was just asking a question, Ethan," Shauna justified, avoiding his jade green eyes.

"I take it you haven't given it much thought?" Johnson directed his attention towards Ethan.

"Nope. I don't really care. School and everything are broken. You memorize information for a test, and you forget what you 'learned' as soon as you hand it in. It's not like that's going to help in the *real* world anyway. You think they get the surgeon ready to scrub into the OR and give them a pop quiz on transitive verbs or whatever the hell? Makes no sense. It's just not how things work."

"And you would prefer…?"

"Whatever it is, it's not that."

"And what's wrong with us staying behind? Don't you think that them having a presentation on how dangerous these woods are should mean that, I dunno, we *shouldn't* be going into the woods?" Shauna argued.

"You're scared?" Ethan pointed out.

"No. They're just legends and myths. They don't even-"

"Scared that you'll get in trouble," he clarified. "You don't care about the legends or anything. You just don't want to sit in detention like Isabella." Shauna didn't respond. "How's that divorce going, by the way?"

Shauna sighed. She didn't want to respond, but she had been secretly hoping someone would inquire, so she would have the chance to express her thoughts. "It hasn't even been that long, and my mom's already with another guy."

"How long?" Johnson asked.

She stopped to think. "I guess it has been a few years or so," she concluded. "It just feels like it hasn't been that long- but also like it's been forever!"

"Who is he?"

"Get this: her *dentist,*" she laughed, hoping to cover up the fact that this was still quite discomforting to her.

"Gross," Ethan responded. "Could you imagine cleaning someone's teeth before you ask them out on a date?"

"He's the dentist. Not the hygienist."

"Like that makes it any better."

"What happens if they break up?" Johnson asked.

"Depends on who's dumping who. If he dumps, she travels twenty miles north for her next cavity. If it's her, he 'accidentally' uses one of his tools to drill a hole right through the front."

"Oh, grow up," Shauna responded. "I need to be happy for them. They make each other happy, and so I have to be happy, and then we're all happy. Besides, they're adults. They can handle it like adults, and I can handle it like an adult."

"You're not an adult."

"I am simply growing into it, and this will help me grow."

"Yeah, sure," Ethan scoffed. "Speaking of handling things like adults, how's that working out for you, Johnny?"

Johnson pressed his lips together. He clearly didn't like Ethan calling him a nickname, especially considering how difficult it is to get people to call him Johnson in the first place. Every time he would have to write his name on an official document, or a substitute teacher would call attendance in school, he'd be subjected to the name that he despised. But he cared very much about satisfying Ethan, and he didn't have the courage to tell him otherwise anyway. And so, he simply ignored and continued on. "How's what working out for me?"

"Handling things like an adult. You know. The *dare*?"

"What dare?" Shauna butted in. "Johnson, you didn't tell me about a dare. Did someone dare you to do something?"

"Bethany Davis and her gang dared Johnny to streak across the football field in nothing but his underwear."

"And why would he do that?"

"Because if I don't, they said they'll pull me into the chemistry room after hours and brand me with a hot plate."

"That's not... legal!" She paused, picturing the pain. "You should tell the school counselor! Or wait- if it's after hours, then maybe the police? Or maybe Mrs. Frennenstein-"

"That's not gonna happen, Shauna," Ethan cut her off. "And Johnny, they're not even gonna brand you," he reassured. "They'll probably trip you down the stairs like they did to Ali Husseini." Shauna shot him a look of sheer aggravation, only for it to be deflected. "Or maybe they'll lock you in the gym closet overnight like Susan Kim. Or maybe, they'll crown you the prom queen and-"

"Ethan!" Shauna hissed.

"Shauna, it's okay," Johnson blurted. He had tried to be reassuring, but it came out harsh and frustrated.

"Yeah, it's okay, Shauna," Ethan mocked, aiming the jade at Shauna. "It's not like I-I dunno- cheated on my boyfriend or anything."

Shauna's cheeks felt warm. "I didn't cheat on him!" she argued. "I left him for someone else. They're two completely different things. There's decency." Her voice had decrescendoed to nearly a whisper.

"Decency? You didn't even lock the door before you opened another one," Ethan pointed out.

"Well, maybe he already locked the door, and so I just got rid of the key. Who told you, by the way? I made a point *not* to tell you for this very reason, because I know you're just going to be a thick-headed *jackass*!"

Silence swept over the group, a grin sitting proudly on Ethan's face, and Shauna's face burning with an abashed heat. It suddenly felt as though the very same eyes that peeked through the trees were beginning to close in. The fingers of the branches were lowering, as though they were attempting to pull the adolescents by the skin and rip them inside out, and make a puddle of their secrets at their feet. "These woods are getting pretty thick, aren't they?" Johnson mentioned, in an effort to leave the conversation behind them. "Shauna, you didn't want to go too far, right? Maybe we should turn back."

Shauna halted, crossing her arms tight as though she were squeezing a balloon trying to pop it. Johnson's conversation only gave her an excuse to release the words ensnared between her cheeks. "And it's not like we ever do anything to judge you, Ethan. We never ask about you because you never want to talk about it. So, we respect that. And then you drag us out here and start criticizing our lives, as if we're not human beings who make mistakes. You know, like... human beings!"

Ethan whirled around to face her. He was a decent amount taller than her, so his stature naturally became intimidating. He stepped forward, and she found her leg catching her weight behind the other. "You're getting pretty defensive," he noted. "You must've cheated with someone real juicy." He took another step forward. She took one back. "Who was it?"

"Ethan," Johnson called, trying to break up the interaction.

"It wasn't cheating," Shauna pressed by emphasizing each word on its own to indicate her tenacity.

"Ronan Basco?" Shauna shook her head. "Dewey Delsea?" She shook her head again. "Harrison Bellchop? Carlos Hernandez? Tell me if I'm getting close. Owen Taylor?"

"Ethan!" Johnson shouted. But at the same time, Shauna decided she had had enough.

"Alex Daley," she snapped, her voice not necessarily louder, but rather sharper as though she hoped it would cut away at any response he would offer.

Ethan looked at Johnson. "Who the hell is he?"

"*She*," Shauna corrected. "Alex Daley is a girl in my trigonometry class. You don't know her because she doesn't waste her time talking to assholes like *you*. So yeah, you don't know her, and I think that's for the best because *I* don't even wanna know you. You just show up one day out of the blue and decide that-that you're just going to tear our lives apart? Huh? What the hell is wrong with you? You're lucky that Johnson and I have been so welcoming to you when you've only been this- this-this huge jerk!"

In her mind, Shauna felt as though she had set him straight. She pictured him becoming a redeemed member of their group, talking about what college he was interested in going to, or sharing parts of his life with them. She imagined herself growing comfortable enough to actually introduce Alex to him one day, and then the four of them getting along with each other. Maybe they'd keep in touch after they graduate and come to each other's weddings or look forward to seeing each other at high school reunions. In the best scenario, perhaps they would even meet for coffee on occasion to catch up on the latest happenings in their lives. But clearly, Shauna did not know Ethan well enough.

He smirked at her, his smug expression piercing through her like fingernails under skin. "Oh, I see what this is about," he started.

Johnson realized what was about to happen. "Ethan," he warned. "Ethan, cut it out."

"This isn't about me or about you or about Alex what's-her-face." He leaned in to the point where she could smell his hot, stagnant breath brushing her nose as he concluded, "This is about Johnson."

Johnson opened his mouth to respond but found curiosity possessing him. What was Ethan talking about? "You're upset because I came into your lives and butted in between you two. You thought you'd have your chance after Angus, but that didn't happen, did it? And so, you've been dating around to pretend you're okay with it, but you don't really have feelings for these people. Sure, you like them, but is it more than that? Do you actually picture yourself with them in the future? When you go off to wherever the hell you're going? No, you're just trying to hide the fact that you're in love with Johnson and you're trying to cope with the fact that he's not gonna love you back."

To Shauna, it felt as though time was frozen. She felt her heart sinking into her chest like a wrecked ship snapping in half. It took the Titanic close to three hours to sink. She could have sworn she had stood there that long, listening to endless swan songs and fleeing fleets. And despite the clamors of those around her trying to determine what action to take, whether it be to file into a boat, dive into the glacial waters swallowing the ship, or simply wait and allow fate to run its course, she found herself petrified, uncertain of what to do next. Should she turn to Johnson? She feared what would happen should she look into his eyes, whether he would tell the truth or not. Should she look at Ethan and see the narcissistic expression on his face, his lips pressed inward into a smirk, and his eyes demanding attention? She feared her anger would consume the best of her.

And so, she pushed Ethan away from her. As he stumbled backwards, surprised, not falling but rather losing his balance, she stormed off into the woods without them. She wondered whether or not it was characteristic of her to avoid confrontation and if it made her better or worse than her sister, Isabella. She didn't care anymore. She simply couldn't be around these two.

"Shauna!" Johnson called after her. "Shauna, come back!" he begged, his voice fading into the distance. "Shauna, it's not safe!"

She wiped stinging tears away from her face, wondering how long they had been there. Did Ethan notice them? She didn't care. She trudged onwards, her feet catching on twigs and broken branches, their fingers trying to direct her back to the conversation from which she just walked away. The eyes were enjoying the drama like a cat toying with a shrew. Deep within the depths of her stomach, she felt the need to turn around- as though the forest was beginning to swallow her, and if she continued onward, would be digested and long forgotten. She pressed onwards anyway. Whatever was waiting for her there needed to cool down before she could return. *She* needed to cool down before she could return.

But as she was escaping, she could hear the footsteps of someone else behind her. "Shauna, come back," he called. "Shauna, please!"

She hoped she could outrun him or that he would tell her his feelings while she continued to storm away so she could avoid them as they came. Were they far enough away from Ethan yet? She wasn't certain and so she continued, half hoping that Johnson would continue to follow her, but also hoping that he would just leave her alone.

This is ridiculous, she thought to herself. *I can't just keep running away from this forever.* And so, she stopped. She took a deep breath and turned around to face the boy behind her.

Understanding the basic structures
of the human brain

By Justintine Wade, PhD

The human brain is an incredibly complex organ that is still full of mystery, regardless of the copious amounts of research that have been conducted. Humanity's greed for knowledge will continue to come up with questions regardless of what we already know, and just as we strive to better understand ourselves and the world we are in, the brain will continue to pose inquiries about what it means to exist. But still, this does not hinder us from trying to establish a comprehension of what the brain consists of and what each part contributes to our functions as human beings. And so, with that, we begin a brief overview of the brain.

The Cerebrum

The most noticeable features of the brain are the signature ridges as though someone had coiled it into the confines of the skull. This section of the brain is referred to as the *cerebral cortex,* whose wrinkled appearance can be attributed to the mountainous *gyri* (singular: *gyrus*) and cavernous *sulci* (singular: *sulcus).* The gyri and sulci's unique structures optimize the surface area within the brain and contribute to the brain's growth and change, a process referred to as *neuroplasticity* Evolution works its hardest with neuroplasticity and is able to enable the brain to recover from any injuries or diseases that may influence brain function. These gyri and sulci eventually create the different sections of the brain, referred to as *lobes,* and divide the brain into two different *hemispheres.* The separation between the two hemispheres is referred to as the *corpus callosum,* which exhibits an understanding between the two hemispheres and demonstrates extreme distress and confusion of the brain's comprehension when severed. This will be explained further in a later chapter. Interestingly, one side of the brain controls the actions of the opposite side (i.e. the right side of the brain controls the left and the left side of the brain controls the right).

Exploring the lobes, we first examine the frontal lobe, located at the front of the skull, as indicated by its name. It controls more complex thoughts such as personality, motor control, thinking, reasoning, and problem solving. It is important to note how much the frontal lobe has broadened with human evolution, and let us attribute our interesting advancement with technology and social relationships to this lobe. The frontal lobe can also contribute to the understanding of emotions, regardless of how complex these emotions might be, such as empathy. Attention is also impacted by the frontal lobe, which means that an attention span might not be so easily preserved in a smaller frontal lobe. The reward system and ability to learn through classical and operant conditioning is located within the frontal lobe, allowing the brain to continue to learn throughout its endeavors. Finally, speech and language production can be found in the frontal lobe within the *Broca's area,* but speech and language comprehension is located in the *Wernicke's area* in the rear temporal lobe.

The temporal lobe is located behind the frontal lobe at the temples and contributes to language and speech comprehension, as previously stated. Within the temporal lobe, one may locate the *hippocampus,* which is responsible for memory and learning. One of the more interesting structures within the temporal lobe is the *amygdala,* which contributes to fear response, resulting in the classic fight-or-flight (or freeze, as some claim) reactions in a dire situation. It is associated with core memories and can be acknowledged for enabling us to learn from our mistakes and understand how to survive instinctively. Without a structure such as the amygdala, perhaps we would never have learned through evolution and societal teaching of the dangers of the world, which would have brought humanity to an uncertain (but most likely horrible) death. When fear is perceived, it is thanks to the amygdala, which pushes the brain to its limits and ensures that the body is kept alive by all means.

Lying in the brain's center and above the temporal lobes, we find the parietal lobes, which are responsible for sensory information. This can include the unique differentiation of touch, the complex exploration of taste, and the dichotomy of temperature. The parietal lobe works strenuously in conjunction with other organs of the body, such as skin and nerves, to guarantee that all sensory information is properly received. Pain can be associated with the parietal lobe because of this, and helps us understand that whenever we are in pain or experience a physical trauma, it is perceived within the parietal lobe. Pain is a feeling of discomfort experienced by (nearly, I expect) everyone on the planet and is essential to ensuring our safety. This can pair with the amygdala and fear response to make certain that we remain as free from harm as possible.

Finally, at the back of the skull, we can witness the occipital lobe, which is the main location of visual processing, as indicated by the name. This is where the *visual cortex* resides, which processes our visual information. Some may argue that this is a more important structure to the brain than the others, but this can be disagreed with regard to the fact that those who are blind are still able to live their lives without perfect sight. While sensory information is important to our well-being and ability to comprehend the world around us, there are other factors within the brain that provide us with experiences that cannot be put into words or images. These are the structures that understand, not necessarily what it means to be human, but rather what it means to be *alive* at the end of thousands of years of human evolution.

The Cerebellum

Beneath the cerebrum, we locate a structure called the cerebellum, which imitates a smaller version of the cerebrum and, when observed in cross-section, can demonstrate the structure of a tree, hence its nickname, "The tree of life." The cerebellum is responsible for muscle movement, coordination, posture, and balance. An understanding of the cerebellum's effect on a creature can be known through felines- cats with *cerebellar hypoplasia*, also known as "Wobbly Cat Syndrome", are identified by a smaller or underdeveloped cerebellum. In turn, these cats have difficulty maintaining balance in their movements. The cats can live happy lives, but simply face adversity in movement.

Thalamus and Hypothalamus

The *thalamus* is located in the center of the brain and can be deemed responsible for consciousness, sleep, and alertness. Protruding from the thalamus in all directions are nerve fibers that are responsible for the exchange of information to other portions of the brain. Every sensory system is able to be received within the thalamus and then sent out to the primary cortical area of the brain. In terms of consciousness, the thalamus is able to regulate arousal, awareness, and activity. Damage to the thalamus can result in a permanent coma.

Beneath the thalamus is the *hypothalamus,* which is most important in linking the nervous system to the endocrine system. This is achieved through the *pituitary gland,* which is a pea-sized gland that regulates physiological processes and excretes hormones to regulate the body through stress, growth, reproduction, and even lactation. The pituitary gland is also linked to the induction of puberty due to the amount of hormones being released in order for it to commence.

The Brain Stem

The brain stem is exactly what the name indicates: it is the stem of the brain and connects the cerebrum to the spinal cord. It is a continuation of the thalamus and consists of the medulla, pons, and midbrain.

Starting at the base, we have the *medulla oblongata,* which is responsible for autonomic- or involuntary-functions such as breathing, heart rate, blood pressure, Circadian rhythms, and sleeping cycles. The very aspects that establish us as humans and allow us to breathe and reside on this planet are because of the medulla. The blood flowing through our veins and the oxygen circulating through our lungs are able to be processed by the system because of the medulla. To conclude, life exists because of the medulla.

Working our way up, we locate the *pons,* which is found primarily in humans and other bipeds. The pons is responsible for conducting signals from the brain between the cerebellum and medulla. It can be seen as a messenger of sorts between the base and the rest of the brain.

Finally, at the top of the brain stem is the *midbrain,* the most forward portion of the brain stem. It is associated with motor control, vision, hearing, arousal, and temperature regulation. The midbrain is able to relay information for the rest of the brain in terms of hearing and vision (which is appropriate considering its position in relation to the rest of the brain).

Chapter Five

Although this current shock has left me full of anguish, I would suffer it all again, arduously to live another life with you.

She wasn't old enough to remember when her sister was born, but her parents always told stories about how hilarious her jealousy had been. With the pressing of a bottle to the baby's lips, she would press herself against her parents' legs with the hope that they would take a look at her preschool project. "What a beautiful baby we have," they would coo to each other, and the only thought that would arise was the question of whether or not *she* had been beautiful herself.

Her name was said to mean "darling" or "beloved," and this was the exact representation that Macie was subjected to her entire life.

***

She could tell her body was lying on something hard and uneven, but she had difficulty pinpointing her location at that very moment. The world around her smelled of sap, and her clothes were growing sticky and began to cling to her skin. She felt the adrenaline flooding. Within a few moments, it would trickle away. She would be left to her own devices, and her body would abandon itself. Her arms and legs were numb with pain– more adrenaline. She couldn't help but draw her attention back to her soaked clothing. She couldn't tell what substance flooded the cloth. It was entirely possible that it was a combination of anything her body was able to produce. Still coming to her senses, she could not smell what it was. *What a pathetic state I must be in,* she thought to herself, and a realization hit her that how comforting and distracting it was to hear her own voice in her head.

Whose voice was it usually in her head? Did she have an inner monologue? When she thought of what she was going to say, did she hear it in her own voice first, skipping through the words as her mind was quicker than her lips, or did the words simply appear, generated deep within the Broca's area without a moment's hesitation? Is that who your conscious is? Or are morality and speech tucked away into different files of the brain, only communicating through the fax of neurons sticky with axons and dendrites? Why was she thinking so hard about the brain?

She raised a shaky hand to her head to find it entirely wet. She pulled her fingers back to see them drenched in crimson. But this did not alarm her. Someone inside of her was pulling the reins back and demanding her to remain calm. Or was it indifference? She felt herself drifting out of consciousness as though a movie was connected to her vision.

***

"Mom, I wrote a story today!" she announced to her mother as she was being picked up from school. "It's about-"

"Your sister is sick," she hushed. "We have to take her to the doctor's, so we're not going home right away. Do you have everything you need to do your homework? We might be there a while."

"What type of sick?"

"Don't know yet, but that's why we're going to the doctor. She hasn't been able to keep food down all day."

"Can I read my story to you?"

"Macie," her mother began, and grazed her forehead with her hand. "I really don't have the time and patience for that right now. Can you just... color or something? Please. Just give Mommy some space."

She chose not to respond. It seemed like her mother didn't want a response from her anyway. She would try to write more stories to pass the time. Perhaps letting a stream of words flow from her mind onto paper would calm her. It would certainly keep her company and enable her to insert her own characters, who were clearly iterations of herself, into different worlds and send them on adventures she would never even dream of taking on in her life. She wasn't sure where these stories came from- she liked to picture a tiny office in her brain with each desk holding a tiny version of herself. They would write away and send their drafts to their boss, and only the best papers would make it up the chain until they eventually drifted out of her mind and onto paper.

Her mother would simply have to wait to hear her original story. She placed it on the floor before her in the waiting room of the doctor's office. Her mother filled out paperwork in regards to her sick daughter and allowed young Sheryll to toddle over to her sister. She was in the middle of scribbling a sentence on her paper (or at least trying to press a solid line while the paper pressed against a soft carpeting) about a dragon and the princess who would save the knight from the castle- that would be quite a twist! And then vomit splattered all over the papers- the original and the current stories. Pencil in hand, she pulled herself away to ensure she wouldn't receive any of the mess from her sister. There was her story in front of her, drowned in rancid ruins. Tears invaded her eyes, each droplet a soldier ambling into war. Her heart felt as though it had jumped off the tallest skyscraper. And then her throat felt as though it was expanding and tightening at the same time. Her whole body was a disaster, like she had never felt before.

"Sheryll!" she cried. "Look what you did!"

***

As the blood seeped out of her limbs and torso and even her face, it flooded from her brain. One might expect this would mean less activity, but in truth, it meant more. Different areas ignited with action- the hippocampus, the amygdala, the thalamus. Everything she could have possibly experienced in her life was now overwhelming her. When a human's body plays against itself, they are generally rendered unwell. The body will do whatever it can to serve as a guardian to itself and its master. These overwhelming responses were not in bad spirit but rather in protection. Her brain worked in overdrive trying to tend to her shattering pain, and manage her fear responses. It was almost as though it did not know she was dying, but rather was a trauma surgeon at the hands of a gruesome surgery slipping out of control.

What was it trying to heal? What would reliving memories accomplish in the moments of severe distress? Was it a coping mechanism? Perhaps a distraction or method of calming? What would numbing her from her pain achieve if it was not there to remind her body to never normalize such a stimulation as this? Was she worthy of the numbness and the promises that it would bear, pressing a finger to its lips as though it would silence her as well? And how would fear assist her if not to force her into herself and live in these moments and the moments of the past, and perhaps even moments of the future? Would it replay every possible outcome of this situation and stick her eyes to the very thing that killed her?

All of these darting thoughts were there only because oxygen had failed to deliver its life to her brain. But that was not her fault, was it?

***

Birthday parties are tough when one is younger, as one does not always have a say in who is to be invited. Her mother, for example, had invited anyone whom she could possibly have known. Many would claim this to be a victory or a point of bragging, and perhaps it was originally. Family and friends gathered, many of whom she could hardly remember since they had only seen her when she had just been born, or when her sister had just been born. The neighbors had been invited over, and everyone in her class was greeted kindly by her mother to join in the party. She had the image burned in her mind of all of these people gathered in her backyard during this one instance in her life, just for her.

That was until Sheryll took the attention away, as predicted. She had just recently learned some of the lyrics to a recent popular song, which everyone was rather fond of. She knew that should that song come on, it would be the end of her reign and passed down to her sister. And of course, so it did. Some people were dancing clumsily, unafraid to make themselves appear silly. But when they heard little Sheryll begin to sing, they all showered her with attention and love. The adults lowered their drinks to turn their heads in her direction as the corners of their mouths pulled upwards. The kids ran over to see the rendition as close as they possibly could. The family members gushed over how incredibly adorable she was. And only she was angry at the fact that she stole the spotlight with a handful of song lyrics that didn't even complete the song.

"Sheryll! Stop that! It's not fair!" she cried to no avail. "This is *my* birthday party, so they need to pay attention to *me*!"

But no one paid attention even to the tantrumming that hid behind the crowd. That is, except for her Aunt Judy.

"Don't worry, Macie," she reassured. She knelt down to her niece's height. "It'll all return to you eventually. The very same thing happened when your mother and I were younger." She placed a gentle hand on her shoulder. "Here, I brought you something. It's not much- I took it from work just for you."

She handed her a small parcel wrapped in newspaper. She smiled at her aunt and began prying the paper apart from the gift. It was a book. It was not brand new, and it looked as though someone had folded the corners of some of the pages. She imagined it would smell a little like one from her school, but she didn't mind. She actually preferred the scent of a used book much more than a newer edition.

"It might be a little above your reading level, but I bet you'll do just fine." She leaned in a little closer and brought her hand to the side of her mouth to indicate a secret. "It's about brains." She wiggled her fingers and made a sound effect to make it more enticing. "I thought you might like it because I know just how smart, little girl you are."

She smiled. "Thank you, Aunt Judy! I'll read it right away!" She gave her aunt a hug. "Thank you for being so kind to me."

Aunt Judy closed her eyes and smiled, elated to have connected with her niece so well after all these years. "I'll always be here for you, Macie."

***

Necrosis began to invade her cells. It hunted them down one by one and choked them to death, till they outstretched a hand looking for a warrior to prevent the circumstances. Do cells know that they're dying? Do they realize they're part of another world so much vaster than what they perceive? How much space do humans consume in a world such as this? The furthest away a human can see under proper standards. What lies beyond those distances? Something as large as the moon can easily be targeted in the sky, but what about beyond that? What happens to the view of a glistening planet fading into the night sky, disguising itself as another star, light years away?

Are we simply cells upon cells in the universe? She began to wonder and think, and expand on how incredibly minuscule we are in the entirety of the galaxies that hold us. Cells can only be seen with certain microscopes that allow for a view so small, and even within those cells are smaller organelles: mitochondria and nuclei and ribosomes. There is the almighty atom and its multitudes of protons, neutrons, and electrons, but how do we know that's where it all begins? Who's to say there isn't more that lies beyond human comprehension?

And then, of course, there's the question of when it stops enlarging. For so long, humans have perceived their lands to be a rarity that exists in their own societal bubbles. And then with exploration and the establishment of science, we are left with the understanding of solar systems and galaxies and the various makeups of all the worlds around us. We come to understand life and how truly fortuitous it all is that we are able to exist in this very space in this very time. So many phenomenal episodes concur to illustrate this fantastically fragile fabrication that we call life. And so, where does life end and the luckless begin? When it continues to grow bigger and bigger until we have clusters of galaxies condensed into the eye of a needle, what lies beyond? Does it all become reborn into the stability of a proton and continue the cycle? What would become of her cells after they died alongside her? What would become of her body when she's gone?

***

"What are you doing in my room?" she asked as her sister guiltily stood in the corner before the bookcase.

"I was just grabbing something to read."

"You grabbed something last week."

"Yeah, and I finished it," she argued. "You really don't have anything good in here, do you?"

"What do you mean?" she objected. She refused to allow her sister to borrow her books that would most likely never be returned, but she also refused to allow her sister to insult her taste. "These are all classics! These have defined literature as it is today!"

"Well, it's a shame literature had to be boring then so that it can be good now."

"These were revolutionary," she disputed as she wandered over to the shelf to grab one of her favorites. "See this one? The plot has been replicated in so much recent media that it's impossible to *not* stumble across a reference. And this one here!" She picked up another one after setting the first face down on top of the shelf. "This one's use of dialect was originally deemed outrageous- people hated it! And now it's commended worldwide because it took the first step that everyone else was too scared to take!"

"Too bad I'll never read it," Sheryll replied, holding the book she chose in the air as though it were an idea. She shook it to emphasize that she was taking it and left the room. As soon as she was gone, she rushed to the door to close it and ensure her sister would not return to steal another book.

And then she reached under her pillow and was relieved when it touched the spine of her book, rigid with years of rereads. She pulled the book out and stared at the cover with its beautiful diagram of the brain: the base of it an oblong shape that held command over involuntary movement and action within the body, a walnut-like structure rested above it to dictate movement, and the beautiful flower of the cerebrum blossoming above it all. She knew it was much too valuable to place on the bookshelf along with the others. Although she was certain that if Sheryll saw it, she probably wouldn't have liked it anyway. The two of them had wildly different tastes, although it often did not stop Sheryll from stealing her books, and it was likely she would think of this one as "too educational" and therefore conclude it "boring."

She heard her sister's door click closed and knew she would be protected from any further intrusions. She opened her book to the first page, the cover bending before the spine so flexible. *Relevé* (noun)– a ballerina's rise to the tips of her toes as if to display to the world the extents of the durability of the human body.

The first page had become so familiar to her that she imagined she would be able to replicate it in her mind, should she ever be without the physical book itself. And so, she started the first line, a wave of excitement carrying her eyes from word to word, knowing this was something she would forever long to preserve.

***

Blood was rushing out of her body faster than she could account for. Do you account for blood? All that she knew was that she could not feel the cells and platelets gushing out of her wounds, but rather, she knew she felt wet and weak. How long had she been lying here? It felt like centuries, and yet she knew that with the condition she was in, it must only have been minutes. She knew she didn't have much left but the time which she does still have could be another few centuries in itself.

Where was it all? She knew there was a gash across her chest and something on her head. She had already checked her forehead for bleeding and could see from the angle she lay at the blood pooling on her chest. Was there more? Was there something worse than this? She swore that she could begin to smell it in this consciousness, a thick waft giving iron and fear, but she also knew that this could be a fight or flight response, anxiety, or something psychological.

Her fingertips were becoming light. It possessed her fingers as though they were dying before her. She imagined them fading into dust or powder and then rising to the skies above. Soon, she knew, the rest of her body would continue to do the same, slowly reaching her wrists and then arms, and eating their way into her heart. She already could feel it emerging in her toes to consume her from another angle. There wasn't much time left. The tingling in her toes and fingers alarmed her, but part of it relieved her, enticing her that she would no longer have to worry about where she ended and where the rest of the world around her began. Is this what people meant when they said they were becoming one with the world?

***

"So, Macie, how do you feel about your sister getting into Damask?"

She took a deep breath. She knew that today was going to be hard, but she was hoping her family would be mourning too much to ask her such questions. Her uncle stood before her, dressed in a black suit, preparing for the wake. She crossed her arms. Why didn't they ever say anything about her getting into Hedera? It wasn't as prestigious, but it was still an accomplishment.

"Good for her," she responded, short and articulated. She wanted to try to remain pleasant since she knew it was what Aunt Judy would have wanted. But if Aunt Judy had gotten what she had wanted, then perhaps she would be here on this very day, and they wouldn't have to pledge their goodbyes to her motionless body. "I'm not sure how the family is going to pay for it," she continued, not even realizing she had said the words until they hung in the air. "My parents told me that I'm not allowed to leave the area because of tuition costs. So, I'm not sure how she's going to afford Damask."

"I see," her uncle responded, only half listening. "What's she studying again? Law, right? She wants to be a lawyer?" She nodded in response. "She's always been very persuasive. I'm sure she'll do an outstanding job." He placed a hand on her shoulder. "You're lucky to have her as a sister, you know. Just in case you get into any trouble." He winked at her, but she pretended not to have noticed.

69

She took another deep breath as family and friends began to usher into the next room; all pleasantries already exchanged. She knew that it was selfish, but at the moment, she wished that she had been in there, sitting beside Aunt Judy.

***

Her eyes were beginning to fail her. Or was it all in the occipital lobe? Did she hit the back of her head when this terror came upon her, or is this part of her demise? She wished she could draw her fingers to the back of her skull to survey the area, but she was far too weak and her fingers were way too numb. Any efforts would be futile. Or perhaps, she suddenly came to wonder, it was from her old age. She had rushed through life to this point, so fast that she never had the chance to stop and catch her breath. She could have had her sight slowly diminishing beyond her reach for so long that she never truly witnessed it until this moment. She hoped this was the case, but knew in honesty that it was not.

She tried to focus on the branches above her. They seemed to loom overhead like a judgemental swarm winding up to attack. But the longer she stared at them, the more their colors turned to blotches and oblong shapes like a creation of Rorschach. What is reality? How do we become certain that we reside within it? If it's something you can see, are the blind without it? And if it's something we hear, are the deaf short-handed? What makes touching something all the more real if we cannot feel the individual atoms at our fingertips but rather the matter it creates? And how do moments become reality? Memories are simply pictures within our minds that come to fail us every so often. Countless stories surface of eye-witnesses turning in the wrong man due to blips and rips in memory, lies that our brains accrue. If our own minds cannot process reality, how can we be certain we're living within it?

Her eyelids begin to feel heavy, the light of the sky breaking through the branches like a gracious liquid and burning itself into her eyelids so she continues to receive their tease even when she closes her eyes. Is it really light, or is it the fingers of heaven reaching out to take her?

***

"We're sorry, Miss… Crane… but we feel as though your abilities would be more suitable at another company."

She hung her head on the way home as though her entire body was shutting down and falling apart at the news. She had felt so confident earlier. She had put so much into this that she was certain her destiny awaited. For so long, she had felt optimistic that everything in her life would happen for a reason- every step she took, every mistake, every emotion- would lead her in the right direction until she found herself somewhere that would make her happy. She spent so much time at Hedera and acquired as many credits as she could, and this had been the last location that had not yet rejected her.

She needed wine. She knew that coming home to Doug would make her feel significantly better. Hopefully, the two combined would raise her spirits and encourage her to prepare herself for her next step in life. Whatever was coming her way, she was certain that Doug (and wine) would enable her to feel powerful enough to tackle it. Doug had been a true blessing in her life, appearing almost out of nowhere and becoming someone so close to her. She knew that she could trust him and that they were destined to be together.

She fished for the key to the apartment, only for her key ring to pinch her as she tried to pull it out. She let out a sound at the impact but knew that it was not enough to draw blood, and by the next morning, she would most likely forget about it. She inserted the key and turned it. The door opened to a dark room with light shining from the bedroom.

"Doug?" she called, more tired than loud. "I had quite the day. I really just want to have a drink or something." She heard no response but rather a gentle creaking originating from the bedroom. Her heart dropped, and she stormed over to the bedroom and tore the door open.

Doug heard the door and whipped his head around only for his expression to turn to pure guilt. He was on top of a woman whom she could not see. She marched to the bed and yanked the covers off, only to reveal sticky bodies and a familiar face.

"Sheryll?" she cried. "What the hell are you doing?" she aimed at Doug.

"Macie," he started.

"Don't say it's not what it looks like because I'm pretty certain that's exactly what this is!" she accused. She turned her head to her sister. "Get out," she commanded through gritted teeth.

Pulling the sheets with her, she fled from the bed and collected her articles of clothing and then scurried out of the room before closing the door behind her.

"I can't believe you, Doug!" she started. "How could you do this to me? How could you do this to *us*?" But suddenly she was filled with a terrible feeling. It could have been the mixture of the affair and the rejection, but it brewed within her, rotting away at her being until she was left with a deafening precariousness. "What did I do wrong?" Her eyes began to tear up, fluid rushing into her eyes so fast that it blurred the naked man before her. "Why would you do this to me?"

***

She knew that the end was very near. The ringing in her ears was beginning to die down, and the tingling that had begun in her fingers and toes had crept up her arm like ivy trying to reclaim its territory. Her vision was mixing the world around her into a painting in which someone had dragged a wet brush against it. This was the end, and she knew there was no sense in fighting it. She had already decided what seemed to be an eternity ago that she would not fight it. She knew that in reality, she had nothing to fight for. *Is this something to be ashamed of?* She wondered to herself. *Is it wrong to wish this upon myself?*

Certain humans would claim that it's against God's will. She had been raised in an odd concoction of religion. Her parents had been raised religiously but she had only received a diluted version of all of the customs. Was God something she believed in? Was life really all part of His plan? She thought of the ups and downs of her life, and imagined a man sitting at a table while resting on a cloud in the heavens. He dipped a pen in ink and began to scribble out words to draft the story of her life. Is this what He intended? Is this how her story was meant to end? Who would write a story of a woman subjected to so much neglect and pain, always second-best to her sister, who may or may not have deserved the glory?

No one would ever create a character like that. Perhaps if she were a secondary character in another's life, she would see herself with this fate, but she knew that she was seeing

73

blur through her own eyes. This was the life she was subjected to.

But then something washed over her. She felt her heartbeat begin to slow down as though she was entering a final slowing. And then there was an overruling calm that painted her entire body. The tingling had reached her chest, and she imagined herself brushing it away like dust that had come to rest on her body, that had been sitting far too long in this position. Her eyes were closed, and she could not remember when they had decided to do such a thing. She felt bliss.

Life was warm and full of grace- at least at this very moment. It could have been her body trying to produce something pleasant, sending endorphins like a paint bucket kicked over, but she chose to believe it was something much greater. It was like fresh linens, still warm from the heat of the dryer. *Wrap them around me*, she thought to herself. *I want it to cover me and leave the scent of lavender and chamomile.* Warmth. Does that mean this is it? She lived through it all and then replayed it all again. Had it been worth it? Would she go around again, had she been given the choice? Would she do anything different, or would she make the same mistakes over and over and act surprised when things didn't quite work out her way?

Now was the time to make peace. Did she truly hate her sister for all that had happened between them? She wanted to. She truly did. But she knew that deep down inside, she couldn't bear to bring herself to hatred. She didn't want to be like everyone else, placed on a pedestal and hoping for the glory that came with her presence, or becoming the moon that revolved around her. She was supposed to want something more from the two of them. They were supposed to have a bond like no other two people on this planet as sisters. Was this what she had wanted? Was she just like everyone else?

Was she behind greatness?

What greets you with death? The cliché of a blinding light? The warmth that embraced her? The memories of her life flashing before her eyes like an old movie, frame-by-frame, with the white noise of the projector? She would never live to tell. *Adieu, my love. May we meet above the clouds.*

Chapter Six

You have made me everything I am and shaped me into my ambitions. I can only hope I have done the same for you.

Clara was reluctantly growing accustomed to her father working at home, and the sight of him in his makeshift office was becoming more familiar to her when arriving home from her whereabouts of day. But one day he had to leave for a business trip, and this meant- to Clara's delight- that she would be allowed to spend an entire week with her mother. Luckily, this lined up with a summer break, and so she was not forced to attend school, which only meant more time invested with her mother. She didn't question the technicalities of how her father knew she would be home from her adventure, especially considering how he never seemed to know much about her endeavors whenever she questioned him about them. But that didn't matter to her at the moment. She was simply elated to know she would be spending the week with the scent of oranges and dark, coiled hair.

She was somewhere around eight or nine years old at the time, and so she was growing into a state of independence in the sense of detesting a hovering eye over her shoulder, but still secretly hoping for guidance. Being around her mother again, however, drew her back to a younger age of sitting in her lap and falling asleep in her arms on days when she felt ill. Part of her wished she was still small enough to sit in her mother's lap without having to worry about balancing or discomfort. But there was something a little off about her mother's appearance that she couldn't quite place.

It could've been that her mother had last been away for a month- 34 days to be exact- and plenty could have changed in a month. But this was something that appeared more temporary. She was paler than usual- perhaps her adventure was somewhere colder. Clara imagined her mother alongside penguins and polar bears, wrapped up in a puffy parka to protect against the perpetual puffs of piercing winds. There were bags under her eyes- maybe it was due to jetlag and the fact that she was halfway across the world and her body was still adjusting to the rise and fall of the sun. This was not something Clara had ever experienced for herself, but rather something appearing in her life secondhand whenever her mother would come back after a long trip, and she'd want to greet her right away. "Give your mother some space, Clara," Jim would tell her. "She's… jetlagged, so you'll just have to give her comfort." Her mother was also much skinnier than she had been 34 days ago. She had never been relatively big or small- she was as close to average as she could have been. But now the tiny tummy, which Clara loved to throw herself into for warm embraces, was absent, and her cheeks were hollow, revealing an angular jawline. Clara pictured that she had gone on a hunger strike- something she read about in her social studies class. She pictured her mother standing up for some belief she couldn't wrap her mind around. But wasn't she with the penguins? Perhaps she was representing penguin rights!

Jim seemed hesitant to leave for his trip. Clara imagined it was because he was so thrilled to have all three of them home, finally, at the same time, only for him to embark on his own journey. He had explained to Clara that this would help him get a promotion, and that he was really hoping he would get it, but she was too busy thinking about all of the games she would finally get to play with her mother. Before he left, Jim brought his wife into the other room and started whispering to her. Clara knew that this meant their conversation was not for her ears, but she couldn't help but sneak to the other side of the wall to listen.

"I just don't think I can do this," her mother was saying, driving confusion into Clara's mind.

"You'll suffice," Jim responded. "One simple week and then you can return to... whatever the hell you do." Clara's ears perked at the sound of the word "hell." She was always taught it was impolite to use that word. This only made her angrier at her father. Why was he leaving them behind? "There's no choice here," he told her. "My plane leaves at 5. The neighbors are available if you need extra hands."

"The neighbors hate me."

"No surprise there."

"Jim," she urged. "Jim, please don't make me do this. If not for me, then for *her* sake."

Silence.

"I'm going to be late."

The footsteps began crescendoing, and so, Clara ensured she would appear at the front door to bid her father farewell. He gave her a hug and a kiss, and then he was on his way, silence preceding the locking of the door.

Her mother spent the entire first day bedridden- or more specifically, couch-ridden. Anhedonia (noun)- the inability to feel pleasure even in the smallest joys. Clara told herself it was just the jetlag again, and wondered when her mother would be ready to play with her. She timed the minutes her mother slept, wondering how long she could possibly be asleep for. Her concern grew the closer it got to dinnertime.

Usually, Jim would begin preparing dinner at sundown and have it ready within half an hour, an hour if he was feeling really fancy. But the sun had gone down, and her mother was still dormant, and so Clara began to wonder whether she should prod her awake or not. Perhaps this jetlag had her preparing meals at a later time, but she figured she would inform her mother of the dusk.

"Mom?" she whispered, hoping she wouldn't startle her. She scooted closer, afraid to raise her voice any more. "Mom, I'm hungry," she said. She realized in this moment that her mother no longer smelled of oranges, at least not in this particular moment. Between the sickly complexion, inkblots beneath her eyes, and the new scent of something reminiscent of burning wood, was that even her mother at all?

Her eyelids lifted as though weights were strung to her eyelashes, and she watched her irises quiver, as though she was rousing on an operating table, her veins full of adrenaline and apprehension. Clara grabbed her arm, hoping this would warm her in some way. Her mother's arm snapped away, and she sat up instantaneously, grabbing hold of her surroundings. She turned to her daughter. "Oh, Clara!" she sighed in relief. "Clara, Clara, Clara! I-" Something came over her all of a sudden, and she scrambled off the sofa and into the bathroom, throwing the door shut behind her. Clara rushed behind her and stood at the closed door, listening and hearing the horrid retching echoing in the toilet bowl.

It was obvious that her mother would not be providing any dinner tonight, and so Clara rummaged through the pantries in search of something she knew how to prepare. She managed to find cans of soup and figured this would be perfect, considering the condition of her mother. She had never used the stove before and was afraid she would get in trouble if she didn't ask first. She returned to the bathroom to ask her mother for permission, but was simply told, "Leave me alone!" and so, she decided that perhaps it would be more effective to prepare the soup now and worry about privileges later.

The rest of the week continued like this. Clara was hoping that the illness, whatever it was, would pass through, but her mother spent the majority of her time in the bathroom. Clara would prepare food as she needed it, often sitting alone at the table, quietly taking her life by the spoonful. Should she ever try to approach her mother, she would be shooed away. Clara had no idea whether she preferred the shooing that was a false haste or one that was uninspired and lethargic. She only hoped she would be able to feed her some, and on some days she would accept it, and on other days she would only be dismissed.

When her father finally came home, it was close to midnight. It had been a long week- in the eyes of an eight or nine-year-old, it felt almost like a month. Clara could tell her father was trying to make a quiet entrance, so as not to awaken her, but she was restless all week. She scurried downstairs to greet her father. She had anticipated that he would be worried about her mother's condition, but she was mistaken.

"You're joking," he stated, although it sounded almost as though it could have been a question. "Where is she?" he demanded, and Clara pointed towards the couch where her mother resided. Clara observed as her father marched over to her mother, and in this moment, it was as though she was seeing her for the first time. The circles under her eyes had deepened and darkened, her skin now resembling something closer to Clara's. Her cheekbones were well beyond defined. She was a skeleton of a woman.

He tore the blanket off her body. "This is too far, even for you!" he clamored at the woman, now shriveled on the couch as she adjusted to the cold air clinging to her bones. "No, it's my fault. I never should have let it get this far! I shouldn't have trusted you to do this! How could I have let this happen?"

Clara couldn't tell if he was speaking to her or himself. She didn't understand why he was so distraught over her mother's illness. "Dad?" She called his name, hoping it would bring some sort of clarity or shed of light on his madness.

"Go to your room, Clara," he demanded.

"But I-"

"Go to your room!" He grabbed his wife by the wrist and pulled her up. Clara was afraid that he might hurt her and stepped closer as if her youthful body could protect her against her father. He turned his head to her. "Now," he ordered through gritted teeth.

She turned and ran away, leaving behind her father and mother. She lay awake in bed that night, listening to the two argue outside the house. She could not hear specifics as the walls of the house muffled their vocabulary, but she knew that whatever was happening was terrifying. She wished she didn't have to endure it alone.

Clara had not even realized that the last time she would see her mother was the last time after all. Perhaps she would have done something different that night. She comforted herself with the projection that she may have found courage deep within her, but she knew that in candor, she would have just stared and observed everything as it unfurled before her, uncertain how to respond. Years later, she would find herself repeating that night over and over, perhaps even comparing it to the night above, trying to pick apart the details like forensics and determine what had been the cause of death. She would never know.

She was twelve years old that night. Her mother had been disappearing for longer periods of time, and often when she returned, it would result in more arguments between the parents. She would always be sent to her room while they shouted, the walls protecting her from their harsh judgments and comforting her, allowing her to know that while she was being forced to her room, this was no punishment. It was up to her to decide whether to believe them or not. Despite the routine of their unavailing wailing, Clara found herself remaining, what she chose to call, optimistic. She would picture her mother coming home- during the day this time- and her father greeting her with an embrace and a kiss. She could imagine pink roses adorning the table, the perfume drifting across the kitchen. Intoxicating. Arriving at night guaranteed an argument. She replaced shouting with love and pictured this being the solution to their problems. Maybe they would both treat her to a family embrace as she found them. They would spend their time with her and listen to what she has to say, and they would tell her that they love her oh so much.

But this never happened. The roses placed once on an anniversary months earlier had wilted, the dust and shriveled petals lying at the base of a vase. Every day grew further from the blush it once was. And that night, when she was twelve years old, she had decided that she would finally listen in on what they were arguing about. She was older, now, so it was possible to her that she would be able to alleviate their anguish.

Her mother came home at night, as expected. Clara had already been in bed, but she heard the front door close. She had trained herself to be a light sleeper to assist in her eavesdropping, and so she hopped out of bed and snuck to the bathroom window, while her parents stood on the patio outside.

"What do you need the money for?"

"You see-"

"No! I know what you're doing! When have you ever used the money for something useful? When have you ever used it on someone other than yourself? Used it on our daughter?"

"You don't understand."

"I understand perfectly fine! You think she's just not going to notice? You come home after *months,* and for what? Money? You're not getting any of it. You don't work for it like I do. I had to take work home just so you could- so you could do *this*?"

"Maybe I don't need your money. Maybe I'll just take some from the fund."

"Don't you *dare* touch that! That's not yours! We *wanted* her to go to college, remember?"

"Why? So, she doesn't wind up like *me*?"

"So, she doesn't wind up like *either* of us!" he hissed back.

"Jim," she tried to soothe. The sound of something almost inhuman, with a splash of her father's voice, gargled.

"Jim?" Urgency flooded through her voice. Clara heard a thud. "Shit," she rasped. The front door tore open, and Clara watched as her mother rushed in. She aimed towards the master bedroom and, after a few moments, appeared with money in hand. She swiftly slid the bills from one hand to the other as she counted under her breath. And just like that, she disappeared into the night. Somehow, Clara knew this would be the end of the conversation, but she refused to let it be the end of her father.

She hurried outside to find her father collapsed on the floor, clutching his chest. "Clara," he wept. "Clara, I'm so sorry."

***

There's something about the sound of another human being that is entirely familiar to one's ear. Whether or not language or any vocalization for the matter is used, something about the clamor of a human gait is indistinguishable to the ear. Perhaps this is the reasoning of how Clara was able to determine that she was not alone in the forest. The thick trees and their what appeared to be eons of rings circling their cores occluded her vision, but she was still able to detect company. The uneven underfoot could easily make a bungler of a ballerina, but Clara's familiarity with hiking in general gave her the upper hand. A fierce wind wove in between the trucks of the surrounding trees, warning- or perhaps threatening- the approaching dusk. The trees were too thick to be disturbed by such a gust, but Clara found some stray hairs contouring her face. But on top of the rough terrain and debilitating winds, one particular human was rather heavy-footed, falling prey to the ever-changing environment around him.

At this moment in time, Clara was still searching for the stream. She knew that it was imperative that she reach it and set up camp nearby in order to survive. She had heard plenty of stories of other campers who dared enter the forest and would have to abandon their partners after they withered away, hypertonic, due to their dehydration. It becomes a hidden predator- one would suspect that in a forest of constant precipitation, hydration would not become an issue. The daytime is when campers begin to comprehend. They would watch as the soggy soil evaporated, creating a thick mist that eventually diminished into the sky, leaving dry dirt and only the smell of a waft of heat. If one weren't careful enough to hydrate enough during the moments of precipitation, the forest would become much too torrid and result in hyperthermia and dehydration.

Clara was determined to deviate from the typical explorer who would tread too far from the stream and eventually become a victim of their own curiosity. And for this reason, Clara was incredibly bewildered to find another human approaching her, by the time he grew large enough in her sight, his older age was obvious to her. She noticed he seemed to be mumbling something to himself, his voice raspy and emerging from his throat in bursts as though something was stuck in his lungs.

"Fancy meeting you here," he grumbled, still a decent length away, but not so far away that she wouldn't be able to hear him. "This weather is just awful."

"Pardon," she began. "Do I know you?" She thought it to be awfully strange that someone would approach her in this manner, especially considering how she didn't really know anyone besides her father and Jessica Heathers. She contemplated whether he could have been one of Jessica

Heathers' many ex-boyfriends, but knew that this man was much too old to have been one.

"No, but I'd like to know you," he offered. Clara couldn't believe what she was hearing. She felt a sudden pang of discomfort, although she knew that she truly wouldn't have been comfortable around this man, whether he was familiar or not.

She tried to think of a way to politely let him down, but figured that he didn't deserve such manners, being that he approached a random woman in the woods and made the impression he had. But he continued before she had a chance to respond.

He finally trudged his way in front of Clara. "I'm Doug," he introduced, holding a hand out.

Clara looked down at his wrinkling hand and looked back up at the man. *Old enough to be my father,* she thought to herself. *Maybe even older.* "Clara," she responded, keeping her hands fixed on her backpack. "What are you doing out here?" she questioned. She thought about the high death rates and disappearances that accompanied the forest and the mountain. She had personally been researching and training herself for this trek. Looking at the man before her, she doubted he could say the same.

"I'm looking for a landmark," he explained.

This sparked a bit of interest, not enough for her to regret not shaking his hand, however. "The river?"

"The river? No, I'm looking for the ravine. Heard it's a lovely sight to see. Wanted to see it for myself."

"It's just you out here?" Clara asked him, realizing how few people had seen the ravine. Those who were able to return did speak of its beauty and wonder, but strongly advised against others witnessing it for themselves.

"Just me," he told her. "But I am open to company."

"I prefer to hike on my own, thank you very much," she responded. She wanted to end the conversation here, but he didn't seem keen on allowing her to leave.

"What brings you out here?" Doug took half a step towards her as if in desperation."I have my own accounts. And I'm sure you have your own as well. Better not allow us to interfere with each other, now." She began to walk away, but he stepped even closer.

"And those accounts don't have anything to do with having fun, now, do they?" He reached out to touch her arm. "Isn't that why we do anything at all? We just wanna find a little joy in life now, don't we?" He crept in closer. "Find other people who also wanna have some fun. Have some fun together." She glared at him, trying to make it obvious that she wanted nothing to do with him.

"Well, I must not be like everyone else because I'm not looking for fun. Especially not in a place like this."

"Has anyone ever told you how beautiful you are?" he deflected. "Such smooth skin. Gorgeous color, too. Where are you from?"

"Nowhere you would know," she retorted, trying to pull her arm away from him, questioning how she had let him hold on for so long.

"Try me," he challenged. "Tell me all about you. I'd love to hear your stories and about your life. I bet you had it easy, didn't you? Everyone must've given you whatever you wanted with a face like that, isn't that right?"

"You have no idea," she responded. "And if my face could get me what I wanted, it certainly wouldn't be looking at you."

"Hey, now." He moved in to try to grab her arm again. She pulled away. "Don't be like that now." He reached out for a lock of her hair that had been torn free by the wind. "Would you look at that?" he murmured to himself. "What a perfect curl. You have such beautiful hair." He snaked his way far beyond her comfort zone. He stretched the curl out and released, watching it bound up and down.

"Leave me alone," she demanded through gritted teeth.

He grabbed her by the wrists. "And what fun would that bring me?" His face was so close to hers now that she could smell his last cigarette. "Too bad you don't like fun."

A scream pierced through the air. For a second, Clara wondered if it had been her. She had never pictured herself to be the type to scream, but then again, she had never pictured herself in a situation such as this. She curiously found herself riddled with regret. She should have learned to prepare herself long ago, knowing she unfortunately did not have power over those around her. She liked to hope that had her mother had stayed, she would have taught her how to handle herself when she came of age. She wondered why her father never did, knowing how protective of her he had become. But that didn't matter at the moment. The scream caught them both off guard.

She tore her wrists away from him and bashed her fist into his left temple. He shuffled to the side and hunched over, but he stayed standing. She wished it had done more, but she decided it would suffice to allow her to escape.

"Stay away from me," she ordered him. Part of her knew that talking to him would elongate their interaction, but she wanted to make her point clear. She would put up a fight if she had to, and she wasn't going to lose.

She realized that he seemed concerned with the scream. He wanted to run towards it. *Perhaps some other conquest,* she thought to herself. "Well, if you're ever looking for fun," he started, admitting to his defeat. "You can just look for me." He turned around and rubbed his temple, trudging away as though he was plagued with a headache for trying to comprehend the size of the woods.

Clara watched as he turned into a silhouette and faded into the trees. She stood there, trying to digest what had just happened to her. She thought through dozens of possibilities in her head of what she would have done had everything progressed beyond her control. She wondered where the scream had come from. Why were they screaming? What horrors lurked in these forests that resulted in so many disappearances and deaths? She hoped that she would live to tell the tale, but more so hoped that should she meet her demise, it would not be at the hands of a man.

Consumed by a flood of thoughts and noting that her heart rate had returned to its resting state, she squatted on the forest floor. She poured her face into her palms and wept. She felt a shiver down her chest as though she could feel the drop of her heart at the realization of what could have happened. *No,* she thought to herself, bearing a sniffle. *This is not how we're going to go down.* She wiped her eyes and stood up. There was no use clinging to a moment she would rather forget. It was time to find the river, and somehow, by some strange force, she felt even more determined than she had been before.

She carried her body taller, as though feigning confidence would bear a difference. She took a few steps forward and then realized something was missing. She pulled her hair back and secured it in place with a hair tie, containing her curly locks in a ponytail. Something about this comforted her, though she couldn't quite place why. *There we go,* she thought to herself. *Time to carry on.*

Chapter Seven

I look to the stars in times like these and see the same twinkle in your eyes, cradled and feel less alone.

"What is it this time?"

The two sisters walked down the street, a distasteful routine, yet one associated with sisterly bonding.

"We're going shopping," Isabella responded cheerfully. "Stop in at a convenience store, grab some things, and then we'll be on our way."

"I'm not shoplifting with you again," she asserted. "Things got too close last time. Besides, I don't get why we have to do this in the first place."

"Mama's got her hands full with Martin. And besides," she turned to look her sister in the eyes. "*We're* not going to be shoplifting this time."

"Something tells me there's a catch."

"*You're* not going to steal anything. We're gonna go in, look around some. You pick up a candy bar or a soda or something. I don't care what it is. You go up and you pay," she explained.

"While you're stealing?"

"See, now you're getting it."

"I dunno," she admitted to her sister. "I just don't feel comfortable doing this. Even if I'm not stealing, I'm still associated with you. We're still walking in and out together."

"Then we don't walk together. I'll tell you to meet me outside when you're done."

"That doesn't make it any better."

"It'll make you look even more innocent." She waited for her sister's response but received nothing. "Is that enough for you?"

She sighed. "What do I get out of this?"

"What do you mean? You get to keep whatever you buy. Oh, I almost forgot." She pulled money out of her pocket and handed it over. "Just don't go over, okay?"

***

She wandered through the aisles of the convenience store, searching for what she felt she was worthy of for enduring her sister's chaos. She had grabbed what her sister had suggested- a candy bar and a soda- perhaps because it was those very words that tempted her. She contemplated grabbing an ice cream treat, but figured it might be a little messy, especially considering how last week the freezer had been broken. But then she saw her brother's favorite candy at the end of an aisle. It had been quite some time since he was treated to one, and she knew it would make his day. They were usually in high demand since all of the kids at school were obsessing over them and a collectible card that came wrapped inside it. She investigated further and noticed that it was the last one in the store.

She quickly added up her soda and candy bar and realized that she was just short of enough to buy her brother's treat. *Maybe they'll be forgiving,* she thought to herself, looking over at the counter. She noticed her sister across the store making different facial expressions at her. It was time to hurry up. She grabbed the candy and headed towards the cashier.

"Just these two?" the inattentive teen asked her as she placed the candy bar and soda on the counter. She nodded her head and placed the money on the counter.

Out of the corner of her eye, she watched Isabella exit the store.

The cashier finished the transaction and handed her the change. They thanked each other, and she started towards the door, only to be stopped by who appeared to be the manager.

"My sister is waiting for me," she managed to say through fear.

"Your sister can wait," the manager responded in an impatient voice. "Now, would you like to return that to its place or would you like to pay for it?"

***

"How stupid could you be?" her mother scolded once she returned home. "I cannot believe you would do such a thing! What a disgrace!"

She was more furious than anything. "Isabella took way more than I did! Why are you mad at me?" she responded, refusing to admit she had done anything wrong at all.

"Isabella, I can expect this from. But you?" She tutted. "Besides, Isabella did not get caught!"

"I did it for us!" she testified. "I was thinking about Martin and when was the last time he had something for himself?"

"He is two years old, Shauna," she asserted. "He has plenty of toys. He does not need candy. He needs to eat like

the growing boy he is, and sugar is not going to help that!"
She pointed a finger at her daughter. "And *you* stealing is not
going to help either."

She looked at her sister and gestured to her mother. "Are
you just gonna let her talk to me like that?"

Isabella shrugged. "I told you that you didn't have to do
anything."

Her arm fell to her side with a slap. She couldn't bear to
withstand this bias between her and her sister. She was
always doing the right thing, unlike Isabella. She couldn't
wrap her head around the fact that she was actually doing
something wrong, and she definitely didn't want to admit to
her mistakes.

"I did it to help the family!" she reasoned once more.
Part of her hoped that making the same argument over and
over would assist her, but she knew deep down that it really
meant that she had lost and there was nothing left to discuss.

"To help the family, stay out of trouble." Her mother
pointed at her to accentuate her point.

"I wouldn't have to if you didn't kick out Papa!" Shauna
attested, hoping this would drive her innocence home.

Instead, her mother came close to her. She hovered over
her by just the slightest amount, but it made all the
difference. She looked directly into her eyes, and she felt her
finger stab at her chest. Her words shot her heart deep into
her stomach, leaving her feeling wounded and sick. She
would continue to hear the words ringing through her mind
as she would sit in her room away from her family, or fall
asleep at night, or when on the verge of morality. Her mother
enunciated well, spitting some of the consonants to make her
point. "You get used to this. He is never coming back."

***

It would be dark soon, and she knew that she should really be getting back to her friends, but she was terrified of what would await her. It already seemed possible that they could be wandering into night, considering the amount of light that managed to squirm through the treelines.

"Shauna!" he called after her. How long had she been running? She was certain she would have shaken him off by now, and yet here he was, only a short distance behind.

She had to stop to catch her breath. She had been an athlete a few years back, but by now she was much out of practice. It was no longer as easy or satisfying for her to exert herself to this extent, and so, she finally took a deep breath and decided to face the fate behind her. She slowed to a stop, placing her hands on her hips and allowing the out-of-breath gasps to flow in and out of her at their command. She tried her best to stifle them as he approached.

"Shauna," he said, finally reaching her. "Shauna, are you okay?"

She wasn't sure how to start. There were a million thoughts flowing through her right now- so many different topics to address. And yet with a million choices at her fingertips, she couldn't find a way to commence just one.

"We never should have come here," she admitted, having known this all along but emphasizing it for the sake of displaying mistakes that were made. "We shouldn't have done this."

"I know, but it's getting dark. We should find Ethan so we can leave and get back to the others."

"Why do you listen to him so much?" she inquired somewhat accusingly. "Why does it matter that you always have to please him and everything he puts you through?"

He paused. "What do you mean?"

"You're always trying to make sure you're on everyone's good side- even people like Ethan. He's Ethan! He doesn't have a good side. All of him is bad. He doesn't care about you, and he sure as hell doesn't care about me!"

"Shauna," he started.

"No, don't 'Shauna' me. You know what I'm talking about. All of the jokes he says and all of the accusations he makes. They're just… he's such an asshole." She waited for his response, but continued after a few moments. "Why do you care so much about what he thinks about you?"

"You say that as though you don't care what he thinks. Everyone wants to be liked. Even by assholes like Ethan." He placed a hand on her shoulder, but she shook it away. "And you know that he does actually care about you. He brought the flare in case we ran into trouble. But really, it's getting dark, and it could be dangerous that we're out here. We should really get back to him."

"How does he care about us? How does anything he does equate to care? Bringing a flare gun doesn't count because he's the one who's putting us in danger in the first place!"

He tried to walk in front of her to make eye contact easier, but she looked away. Eye contact means looking for the humanity in the person and being able to understand their point of view. She was not interested in hearing whatever he was going to say about Ethan. Her mind was set.

"Shauna," he prompted.

She shook her head, aiming her gaze upwards as if to stop the tears that were dwelling in her eyes. "You know they're not going to hurt you," she told him. "They can't burn you with a hot plate because they aren't allowed in classrooms when teachers aren't there. They'll lock the doors. You'll be safe."

"That's not the point."

"You don't have to do what they tell you."

"But they asked me to streak across the football field in my underwear."

"That's-"

"They know what they're talking about. That's the point I'm trying to make. They know what… they know *who* I am."

"Johnson," she soothed. She rummaged for the right words and knew that this was something beyond her territory. She settled on changing the subject instead. "You know I don't see you like that, right?"

He turned to her.

"To me, you're just… Johnson. I- I see you for who you truly are, and that's what matters to me. It's not about who you are or who people think you're pretending to be. You're not pretending to be anyone when you're just walking around. But when you're dealing with these people and acting like streaking across the football field is going to solve your problems, that's fake. The Johnson I know doesn't pretend to let people boss him around."

Silence swept over them as the rising winds interjected their conversation.

"Do you remember how we first met?"

"Shauna…"

"Do you?"

His lips stretched.

"Sixth grade," she clarified with a shy smile.

"Biology"

"No, it was Pre-Al," she corrected. "Biology was when we met the second time."

"Right."

She kept her head turned from him, her pupils seeking the corners of her whites. "You were having such a difficult time with pre-algebra-"

"And you volunteered to help me."

"Mrs. Kinsler *assigned* me to help you," she corrected with another smile.

"But you were still happy to do it."

Her head turned in his direction, but her eyes remained avoidance. "I managed to bring you up to a B- but we rarely even studied. Just goofed around." She felt her smile melt.

He looked away.

"You know, Johnson," she started. "What Ethan said… I don't know how to explain it."

"What part of what he said?"

She fell quiet.

"Oh."

"It's just that… we've grown so close after all of these years. It feels like you're the only person who's ever understood me. We listen to each other, and we know how to make the other smile. I guess what I'm saying is that I've really grown to like you. I think… I think you should give me a chance. We would be good for each other. And if it doesn't work out, no hard feelings. I just… don't want to say we never tried, you know?"

He smiled. "I like you, too, Shauna."

"Huh?"

"You're right. We have grown close to each other. And I like it that way. It would be my honor to take you out sometime." He took her hand. "I never want to make you upset. I want to make it my job to take care of you, whether you need it or not. I want to be there for you."

"You mean it?"

"Of course I mean it." He placed his other hand on top. "Shauna Rivera, will you be my girlfriend?"

She threw her arms around him. "Of course, Johnson. Of course!" The two embraced for some time. She allowed herself to sink into his arms and bury her face into his shoulder. "I have to talk to Alex about things, but I'm sure she'll understand. She's always had… suspicions. But anyway, we should head back now, shouldn't we?"

Johnson didn't respond.

"Shouldn't we, Johnson?" she asked once again.

She pulled back from the embrace to see his eyes now obsidian. It was as though ink flooded his whites and rewrote every detail that made him Johnson. His skin looked as though cockroaches scuttled just millimeters below it, like a thin wallpaper. She feared it would peel away in mildew-stained curls as she watched his face became more unrecognizable.

"Johnson?" she cried, trying to pull away. His arms remained wrapped around her. He smiled, revealing rows upon rows of sharp, jagged teeth. It was almost as though someone had fit an entire jaw of a great white shark into his mouth like dentures, the outline of each tooth squeezing through his gums. As she screamed her next words, she couldn't help but notice another voice shrieking alongside her as though a larynx had been squashed like clay. "Johnson!"

Southwest Heedsboro High School

Dear Parent(s)/Guardian(s) of Francesca Johnson,

We are writing to you in concern about your daughter's behavior at school. Normally, Francesca is an exceptional student, but in recent months, we have been having to address her behavior in school.

It began with the refusal to put the correct name on her homework assignments, which resulted in some confusion on the teachers' behalf. She has also been urging that we address her by male pronouns, which is unacceptable considering how confusing it already is for the teachers and other students to avoid calling her by her own name. Things crossed the line when she refused to enter the female restrooms and instead attempted to enter the male restroom. She is refusing to change in the locker room for gym and is currently using the nurse's office to change. While the nurse has agreed to this, we find this to be unfair to other students and will not be tolerated going forward.

We would like you to address these behaviors with your daughter as soon as possible, as it is becoming distracting to the other students and detrimental to her success in school.

If this continues, we will have to schedule a meeting with you and Francesca so that we are able to properly understand what the causes of these behaviors may be.

Sincerely,

Thom Spetts

Guidance Counselor, Southwest Heedsboro High School

Phone: 521-230

Email: spettst@mail.hs

Chapter Eight

*I can only hope I have served you the same encouraging
service you have done to me.*

"Someone get help!" she cried as she watched the husk
of her friend slumped on the floor. "A teacher, a counselor-
someone, please!"

She was entirely frozen, everything around her caving
in. Passersby were beginning to coagulate, every individual
forming their own thoughts and judgments on what the
outcome should amount to. They all were here to gawk, not
to assist.

She watched as they pulled their elbows back and shot
them forward into his flesh like a slingshot or a bow and
arrow. It mattered not what the comparison was- it was
violent. She could hardly make out his figure between the
bodies surrounding him, each one contributing some form of
anguish to her friend's well-being. A few onlookers would
break off from the crowd and join in, firing their fists
towards him, some of them friends of the original attackers,
others simply people who shared the same belief. All of it
was because of Angus Briar.

"Stop it!" she shrieked, as one of the attacked stood up
to jab his foot into the poor victim's stomach. She threw
herself at the crowd, despite understanding she was
outnumbered. She tried pulling at the shoulders of whoever
was nearest to her, but her fingers slipped off the cotton of
his back. She tried the arms next, using them to yank the
bodies away, but watched as they would fire themselves
back into the crowd. She grabbed one arm only for it to fire

back into her right nostril. Heat engulfed her face, and the scent of iron was now apparent. It didn't stop her.

She managed to tear away one of the attackers and recklessly drove into the crowd, sheltering her friend's bruised body. She knew he wasn't going to fight back, and she couldn't stand to leave the site, fearing that her presence was enough to prevent further damage. And so she decided in the spur of the moment that she was going to protect him, even if it was with her scanty body. She tightened her eyelids and hoped for the best.

Some of the attackers yielded, but others continued. Some tried to pry her away, others attempted to maneuver around her. One simply didn't care and continued to aim his punches into her ribs.

But then the bodies were plucked away one by one until it was just her body lying over his, her eyes producing tears out of dismay and torment.

"Hey," a soft voice called.

She opened her eyes to see a boy standing before her, most probably the one who had taken the suffering away.

"You're welcome," he said, offering a hand to her and hoisting her up. She looked into his jade green eyes for just a second, trying to place if she knew this boy from anywhere, but drew her attention back to tend to her friend and the many bruises that were to come.

***

"No, you're just trying to hide the fact that you're in love with Johnson and you're trying to cope with the fact that he's not gonna love you back."

Shauna pushed Ethan away and tore into the woods alone.

"Shauna!" Johnson begged for her to come back. "Shauna, come back!" He thought of all of the folk tales and myths about the woods and what hid within them. "Shauna, it's not safe!" But she was gone, and there was nothing he could do about it unless he ran after her himself. Instead, he turned to Ethan. "Are you happy now?" he spat at him, accusingly.

"I think that went perfectly, don't you?" Ethan responded with the corner of his mouth curved upwards. He dug his fingers into his wrist.

"You really just gotta push everyone's buttons, don't you?" He pressed his fingers to his temples. "I don't understand what you get out of this. I don't know what sadistic pleasure you're feeling or what, but it's so... so exhausting!"

"So, you're pretending like you didn't know?"

"Know what?"

"That Shauna is in love with you," he stated, clearly demonstrating his lack of remorse for the situation he created.

"That's besides the point of what happened here!" Johnson avoided. "You were way out of line, and now Shauna is– is in the middle of the woods somewhere! What happens if she gets attacked by a bear or something? Or–or if she trips and breaks her foot?"

"Then it's her fault for running off."

"Ethan, it's *your* fault for making her run off!" he cried, gesturing towards the boy in front of him. "I can't believe you! What's wrong with you?"

Ethan just smiled, the one corner of his lips slanting upwards as though it held all of the knowledge of the world. "So, you don't like her back, then?"

Johnson pressed a finger into his chest and articulated through gritted teeth. "I don't know where the hell you came from and why you felt like you had any business intruding on our lives like this, but I hope that whoever hurt you lays in bed at night satisfied that they did a fantastic job screwing you up."

Johnson was surprised to find that these had been the perfect words to say to Ethan. Unfortunately for him, this meant a thicker wave of hatred.

"Fuck you, Francesca," Ethan spat at Johnson.

And so Johnson bashed Ethan across his nose, sending the boy backwards and pressing his palms into his nose. "You don't call me that," Johnson responded, his voice now deeper and dark. Ethan pulled his palms away to reveal crimson. "You don't get to fucking call me that." He looked at him thinking back to why they became friends in the first place. "I don't care if you think I owe you anything. I'm going to find Shauna." And so, he disappeared into the woods.

***

"What's wrong Francesca?"

He tried to find the right words to describe the inner turmoil that had been burdening him for years. He felt as though he couldn't even trust himself, his mind leading him to conclusions he never would have fabricated in a million years. And yet here they were, taunting him and pointing crooked fingers at all of the imperfections he wished he never had. But these imperfections were far more complicated than an unfavorable nose or unsatisfiable amount of hair. It was such a complex topic, and yet one that is dismissed so often, becoming the butt-end of jokes and a picture of adversity.

"You wouldn't understand," he responded.

"Whatever you're going through… You don't have to go through it alone."

He took a deep breath. Surely, he would understand. They had grown so close, despite their rocky start. This man would do whatever he could to make sure he would be happy, wouldn't he? He fell in love with him for who he was, not *what* he was, after all.

"I feel…" He continued to search for the right words as though they were pieces of a jigsaw puzzle, running through the various shapes in his mind and trying to fit them together into coherent sentences. "I feel like I'm not supposed to be a girl," he answered, his gaze wandering away from him.

"Oh," was the response. "I see."

A hand began to lurk. "What are you doing?"

"I'll make you feel like a girl."

"Stop that. Don't touch me there!"

"I'll fix you. I'll make you better again. You just have to let me help you."

"Stop it! Ow! Angus! You're hurting me!" He felt his pants being rolled off his legs, the brisk air brushing against his bare skin. "What are you doing?"

"I'll make you feel like a girl."

***

He carried her limp body as fast as he could. She weighed significantly less than he had expected. He had to get her to Ethan. He wasn't entirely certain if she was still alive. He had tried checking her pulse as he had seen in various movies and shows, but he had never learned the technicalities of how to actually perform it. He realized while stumbling through the woods that he could have placed a hand or ear to her chest, but felt as though it might be an invasion of privacy. Besides, he knew that regardless of whether she was alive or dead, they would need to find assistance, and they would need to leave the woods as fast as humanly possible.

She had been painted in crimson, so much to the point where he wasn't able to determine where it had all been coming from. He was aware that it was staining his clothing, but this was not something that concerned him. He didn't question the lack of a predator at the scene of the crime, but still felt as though millions of eyes pierced their gaze into the back of his neck. He assumed that with wounds this tremendous, something would have wanted to take her body for reasons he refused to think about. He was surprised he was able to find her body at all, considering how vast the woods were. It was as though he had a sixth sense that led him to her, understanding what had happened and exactly what he needed to do.

He saw a figure in the distance and sped up, running faster and clumsily until he was in earshot. "Ethan!" he cried. "Ethan, help!"

The figure turned around and saw the silhouette of a man holding a body, an arm beneath her knees, and another supporting her back.

"Shit," the jade green responded. "What happened?"

"I dunno. I found her like this." He gently laid her on the ground of the woods. "We need help right away."

Ethan swung his backpack off his shoulders and rummaged around to find the flare gun. His fingers felt the smooth texture and saw the bright red of the barrel, and he tore it out.

However, when Ethan looked up, something was askew. Standing before him were two figures. He looked to his side and saw Shauna's limp body gushing away. Her face held a soft expression as though it completely ignored the state of her body. It seemed to be at peace, and in that moment, he realized that the worst had happened to her. He felt his eyes sting with tears, but knew that he had to address whatever was happening before him.

He looked up from Shauna's body to see two identical beings. There were two Johnsons preceding him! They were equally tall, about average height, and wore the same expressions on their faces, clearly worried by the events but equally unaware of the other to their side. Their clothes had the same blood-soaked patterns on them, presumably from Shauna's wounds, the splotches and blotches completely identical down to the shade and the cascade that arose.

His shaking fingers fumbled through his bag, his vision forward but unseeing. In his panic, everything flooded together, but finally he saw it- the unmistakable vermilion. He ripped the flare gun out of his bag and pointed it at the two, uncertain whether it was the correct course of action. Regardless, this seemed to draw their attention to each other.

"Who are you?" the left Johnson asked.

"I'm Johnson. Who are you?" responded the right.

"*I'm* Johnson!" He declared.

"What the hell is going on here?" Ethan interjected, his hands placing a quivering finger on the trigger.

He was at a loss. He had no idea who to point the trigger at, and there were no visual indicators as to who the real Johnson was. He had seen this before in the media, but never actually thought about what he would do in the event of an actual occurrence, since it seemed so obscure to him. And so he opted to recreate what he had seen.

"What's my name?" he asked the two, hoping one would fail.

"Ethan!" they responded in unison, matching the same panicked intonation.

Ethan cursed under his breath. "What's her name?" he asked, tilting his head to gesture at his friend on the ground.

"That's Shauna," they identified, once again completely identical.

Was this a lost cause? He decided to ask one more question to determine whether they would assist in his sleuthing.

"What's the name of the asshole who picked a fight with you the day we met?" He had hoped this more personal question would separate their knowledge from what had happened in the woods. Clearly, there had been some sort of observation occurring, but to what extent was it?

"Angus Briar," they both told him, differing in no measurable manner. They looked at each other simultaneously and decided to elaborate. "He was a year older than us, but he got held back." Their gazes met once again, and so they decided to continue elaborating. "He beat me up because I told him not to call me-"

"Francesca," the Johnson on the right responded.

Ethan aimed the gun at this Johnson and pulled the trigger, a bright red orb surfacing from a puff of smoke and lodging itself directly into the Johnson's chest. He fell backwards, and Ethan ran forward to investigate the body. He looked for any sort of indication of whether the Johnson was really him or an imposter. He found a mole on his neck and looked to the other Johnson to see if they matched, only to find that another figure had replaced the unharmed Johnson.

It was Shauna, hovering over him, wearing a flowing white dress that he had never seen before. He could have sworn she was an angel. She smiled, revealing rows upon rows of jagged teeth.

Ethan aimed the flare gun and pulled the trigger, but to no avail. He bashed his palm into the side of the barrel once, and then twice more quickly. "Get back!" he cried in hysterics. He threw the gun in her direction, but missed. He watched it shatter as it made impact with the asperous ground. He took a step backward, his foot meeting his backpack. His knees, already shaking and weak, buckled, causing him to topple clumsily to the ground.

The Shauna creature took a few steps towards him and knelt down beside him and Johnson. He found himself unable to move. "Thanks for that, Ethan," she sang in a voice that was not Shauna's. He could have sworn he heard another voice mixed in as well- could it have been Johnson's? It plagued his skin with goosebumps as though every ounce of his body was attempting to warn him against the voice's owner. She brushed her finger down his nose, stood up, and then disappeared into the woods.

His heart felt as though it was melting into the acidity of his stomach. He looked down at Johnson, the correct Johnson, and examined his flare gun wound.

"No, no, no," Ethan pleaded, now pulling his shirt up to see clearer.

"Hey," Johnson breathed. "It's okay," he told him, placing cold fingers on top of Ethan's hands. This angered Ethan. He should be the one comforting Johnson, not the other way around! "You did the best you could. I would have shot at me, too."

"I'm so sorry." He tried to hold back tears, but it was as though the dam had broken. This is not what he wanted to have happen. He thought it would be fun to explore the woods. He never would have predicted an outcome like this. "I'm so sorry, Johnson. I'm sorry." He searched for other words but could only find himself apologizing.

"Thank you, Ethan," Johnson rasped, his voice unmistakably weaker. This was it. "Thank you for saving me and Shauna from Angus Briar."

"I'm sorry I couldn't save you this time, Johnson." His tears were slipping down his face onto his friend's body. "I didn't mean to be such an ass- I really didn't. You're just so courageous, and I've always wondered what it would be like to have the strength that you do."

"Hey, hey, hey," Johnson responded. "You don't need to apologize. You don't need to." His breathing became audibly labored. Ethan felt his fingernails dig into his wrist. "Ethan?" he called.

"I'm here. I'm here," he reassured.

"What do you... do you think happens to us after we die?"

"Johnson!" he cried in response. "Don't say that! We're gonna get you both out of here! Trust me!"

"I'd like to imagine… that…" he took a deep breath, and Ethan felt his own heart pause. He watched his chest inflate once more. "I'd like to imagine that one day, I would allow my body to be consumed by the soil it's laid down in. The plants would absorb my nutrients and I'd… I'd become one with the world. I'd become those flowers."

The jade green stung. "You don't have to go, Johnson. You don't have to!"

"I'd like to think… that someday I would blossom into a rose."

Ethan couldn't bring himself to respond.

Johnson took a deep breath before barely vocalizing, "I always hoped you would like me. I always tried-" He inhaled sharply. "I tried to-" His voice trailed away, followed by a long, leisurely exhale.

"Johnson?" Ethan whispered, shaking his friend's shoulder. "Johnson?" This time louder, shaking more frantically. "Wake up! Johnson, I'm sorry! I'm *sorry*!" He leaned over Johnson's body, releasing deep sobs between gasps of air. It felt as though someone was squeezing his lungs, trying to suffocate him. He pulled his head up and looked over at Shauna's body. There was no way he would be able to carry the two of them back, and it was unlikely he would be able to take one. He sobbed harder at the thought of leaving his friends behind and screamed, the sound rattling in his throat. He thought of one final option, quickly identifying it as an impasse when he remembered the flare gun was out of ammo.

And so, he dragged the two bodies beside each other so he could tend to them at the same time. Could he drag one back? What would his peers think happened to them? He couldn't possibly choose between the two. Johnson had always been agreeable and unapologetically himself, although sometimes he would put on a front to appear stronger than he was. Shauna and he bickered often, but it was clear that she cared for his well-being and sense of morality. He knew if it was up to her, she would have him take Johnson back, as she was so selfless.

He wondered what their funerals would look like. Shauna's family was louder, and her extended family was quite close. Johnson had a more diverse family, although there was the chance that if his body were present, they might dress him in more feminine clothes. Who would show up to the funerals? How would they want their bodies to be laid to rest? He imagined Johnson would want a cremation, and Shauna would prefer something more romantic- if there was a way to make a dead body seem romantic. He imagined flowers everywhere, in the room, around the casket, pinned on the clothes of the family and friends. Johnson's ashes would be spread somewhere that would either satisfy him or his family. He knew that at heart it wouldn't matter- just that he was free from the body that abandoned him and caused others to abandon his identity. And of course, he knew there had to be roses.

Unable to make his decision, he slumped on the ground of the woods between his two friends, imagining that they were still alive, their bodies still tepid. He knew that if they were here, they would be able to comfort him. Alas, this was not the case. And so, he had to imagine they were beside him, providing him with the care he felt he never deserved.

"I'm so sorry, guys," he whispered to his friends, as he wondered whether the sound would travel to their brains. He imagined the vibrations ringing through their ears, vibrating and quivering until somewhere along the way it faded away, never reaching its destination.

"Don't be sorry," Johnson would tell him.

"We're here for you," Shauna would say. "Don't worry about us. Just focus on getting yourself out of here," she would instruct. And he knew that she would be correct.

Would people notice that he was even gone? On the field trip, they had to pick partners to ensure no one was left behind. Shauna and Johnson had been partners, so there was no one to point out that they had been missing. He had been partners with Gillian Zimmerman, and he wasn't sure whether he would care whether or not he was missing. Surely, he would care, but would he say anything? Would anyone miss him if he were never found?

He imagined the teachers would have taken the attendance by now. How long had they been gone? How long were they wandering through the woods? He tried picturing the distance between him and the group, but his imagination could not stretch far enough to reach a definite comprehension. He had used the only flare, and so he would not be able to signal to them in any way that he was here. Perhaps he would be able to start a fire somehow, although he had never attempted to do so on his own. He thought of the materials in his backpack- a notebook, some water, a length of rope, and an empty space where his lunch had been- all of it proving to be useless.

Would they leave without him? Would they inform the police and send out a search party for him? Would they dare set foot in the woods with so many myths surrounding it? And those myths- were they true? After the horrors he had just witnessed, it felt as though anything could be possible. What exactly had he experienced, and how had it been the cause of death for not one, but both of his friends? Surely no one would believe him if he had told anyone what he had experienced in these woods. Was he even certain he could believe himself? He thought that perhaps he had some sort of illness that caused him to see things that weren't there or behave in ways he could not comprehend. Were their deaths in his hands?

His thoughts consumed him from the inside out like a parasite digging around in his organs looking for proper nourishment. He hugged his friends close to him, the realization of the day falling deep into his chest as though he was experiencing it again for the first time. Would he die out here along with them? Would he lie here with them until he starved or became dehydrated or came across another one of those creatures, this one looking just like him? Something satisfied him as he thought about a figure of himself killing him. He felt as though it was what he deserved. But he knew that his friends would not want this fate for him and that he must carry on. For the moment, though, he just wanted to lie with them and say his goodbyes.

Chapter Nine

I hope your rest is peaceful, as you have worked far too long to the point where I worried about the rotation of the sun and moon.

He had no idea how he managed to survive high school, and yet here he was, still completely uncertain what to do with his newfound freedom. For four years, he had scavenged for good grades, piecing together whatever would make sense and accepting the Ds and Cs as they came, never trying to work himself too hard, but just barely managing to get by. Whenever he read, it was as if the words tried to escape him. Each letter looked a little more like the next the longer he stared at it. His writing was no better, each sentence carrying words that could be counted on his fingers, with the exception of an occasional run-on or comma splice challenging his habit. He was close to having to repeat his final year; his one teacher was saving him with an extra credit project and stamping his final grade to be only sufficient. And with that final burst of effort, Doug Jenkins knew he would never have to work this hard in his life again.

He never truly had any aspirations. He would listen to others talk about all of their dreams and future plans, but he would only think about the present. How is it that people could focus on something so far away as if the current time had no significance? In truth, one would have to survive the "now" before they could ever carry on into "later." And so he would hear these wishes and dreams and think to himself about something more relevant, like what he was going to have for dinner, or if gas prices were too high that week. He could never keep his attention all in one place anyway, and so he decided one frustrated night that ambitions were not for him.

A local advertisement in the newspaper published a job opportunity at the nearest university, Hedera University, to be precise. Plenty of his fellow graduates would be attending the university, but he didn't mind. He never had any run-ins with any of his classmates, nor did he have any particularly close relationships with them. He was simply sufficient, and a sufficient wage was being offered for a sufficient job. Landscaping was never something he knew much about, but he knew he would be able to learn, should he put his mind to it. It wasn't anything like algebra or literary analyses, and so he knew that he had a shot at whatever they would toss his way.

The trees were in full blossom on his first official day. He would see leaves drifting in the wind, twirling and gliding every which way as if to reach out to another to continue the dance. He had never truly held any appreciation for the blossoms until that very first day when they led his gaze to her. She was pushing her auburn hair into a ponytail, as though a hair tie could command her waves, each one springing back the tiniest bit as she would release tension, only to pull her hair back once again in an attempt to perfect the do. As her hair was pushed around, slight glints of ochre would escape her fingertips, highlighting the ever-changing hue of her hair.

It was almost like a scene from a movie, her body turning towards his with the most graceful gust of wind. In that moment, the world around him had been filled with color, like a man hearing a symphony for the first time. It was as if the orchestra surrounded him, each pull of a bow across a string sending a shiver down his spine and each trill of the flute dancing around his heart. He saw her amber eyes, such a light brown they almost appeared orange, and he couldn't tell what was most beautiful about her. The drifting leaves seemed to mimic the freckles on her face, each one scattering randomly and yet appearing almost choreographed as if the universe was finally falling into place. And even then, he didn't know perfection until he saw her smile.

He had approached her without a second thought and learned her name: Macie. She was a junior at Hedera studying biology, and he was convinced that he was meant to be a part of her life. And so, they planned to meet that Friday night and discuss their lives and how they imagined themselves fitting together, the first chord to the song they would eventually compose together. When the day came, he found himself scavenging through the daffodils he was meant to plant around the campus to present to her, knowing very well where his priorities lay. For once, he actually felt himself looking forward to the future and whatever journey he would embark on with Macie.

When the time came, she arrived with her hair in a simple do; one he pictured her styling in the mirror before swiping a classic red lipstick across her smile. He could not believe she could possibly become any more beautiful from when he first laid eyes on her, and yet, here he was, standing before her and watching her smile emerge as she caught sight of the daffodils. Part of him felt embarrassed, not for the cliche of flowers, but for the fear that they would never be enough to demonstrate his honor in spending time with her.

And so they went to dinner and spoke of their lives, both before and after meeting the other, and where they pictured themselves in ten years: her as a neurologist, perhaps in a prestigious hospital or in a very dedicated future as a neurosurgeon; and him wherever the world would take him. He had relied on chance and coincidence for long enough, and it brought him to her, and so he knew it was dependable. But in truth, he knew that wherever he wound up, he hoped deeply in his heart that he would remain by her side. And with that, he opened the car door for her, walked her to her apartment door, and kissed her, holding his breath and praying their first would not be their last. She smiled at him one last time before disappearing into her apartment, and she didn't need to speak a word to let him know that they would meet again soon.

***

It was the holidays that year when he first met her family. Which holiday, he could not remember, for he was far too nervous that day to think of anything besides making the best first impression he could. Her father was a large man with a burly beard, which was a far darker color than his auburn hair (that hers seemed to mimic). In one way or another, you would always hear him before seeing him- thunderous footsteps clanging from down the hall, or complaining in his raspy voice of a recent news event. Her mother was rather twig-like, resembling an insect he once had seen in an educational magazine at the doctor's office. Her eyes appeared so large in contrast to the rest of her body that they almost seemed to be popping out of her head like a pug. Unlike her husband, she seemed to take up no space, disappearing silently in one moment and then suddenly appearing as though she had been there the entire time. She was an optical illusion- a contortion of reality- appearing in places you could have sworn held vacancy and then disappearing the moment your eyes wound squinch shut.

120

And then there was Sheryll. In another life, he may have imagined Sheryll to be beautiful… In another life. She wore untasteful makeup that tried too hard to accentuate her eyes, and she wore a bright red dress as if she were walking a red carpet, far overdressed. She spoke only of herself, and often those conversations were constructed of incessant bragging. She had skipped a grade, causing her to be a sophomore in college, despite being two years younger than Macie. She attended Damask University, a prestigious law school, and intended to become a lawyer- perhaps even a justice one day. And though she bragged about it, aside from Macie told him about how the grade she had skipped was in primary school, and originally, she had been waitlisted from Damask. He pictured Sheryll as a chihuahua- some may find her adorable, but he did not. Besides, she was all bark and no bite.

Briefly, in the daze between dinner and coffee, Macie had excused herself to the restroom. With her father napping on the couch and her mother disappeared into oblivion, Sheryll had taken to getting to know him a little better. Even though the couch had three cushions with him sitting at the far right, she chose to sit directly next to him.

"You're fond of my sister, yes?" she questioned, as though they hadn't been together for a handful of months. He nodded politely but nervously, still trying his best not to judge Sheryll too soon. "It seems like she likes you, too," she responded, almost in a whisper. He couldn't tell if it was because of her snoring father or the press of a secret. He convinced himself it was the former. She leaned in a little closer. He could smell a stale fragrance from her extended neck. "You're the first boy she's brought home in a long time," she told him.

He didn't even realize he had been looking at her through his peripheral vision. He broke the angled eye contact. "I see," he responded, indifferently. He personally could not imagine Macie being all by her lonesome self for so long, but he also imagined that should she have had someone, she might not have wanted to share this person with Sheryll, who spoke so much of herself. He knew that he personally wouldn't have.

He had hoped that his short response would be enough to indicate to her that he was not interested in having whatever conversation she was attempting, but she pressed on anyway.

"How did you two meet, anyway? Are you at Hedera too?"

He pursed his lips. He knew that Sheryll was incredibly judgmental, from the little interaction he already had with her. He spoke of Macie while she wasn't present- would she do the same to him? "I am… at Hedera, yes," he responded, hoping his answer was vague enough that it answered the question without prompting more inquiries.

"What are you studying?" she asked without hesitation. It was a question he should have anticipated, given the answer he provided, and yet it still managed to take him by surprise. Cogitation (noun)— thinking so deeply about something that you would not be bothered enough to think of the word "cogitation." Her entire family was well-educated, something that he had not grown up accustomed to. What would they think of him?

He could have sworn he could hear the gears grinding in his head, and he was certain that Sheryll could see the smoke puffing out of whatever machine resided in his brain, causing him to make these imbecilic responses. Should he lie and risk the consequences of whatever cacophonous gossip she would make of it, or should he tell the truth and risk the judgement of someone so close to someone he cares about? If he should lie, what would he fabricate? What interests did he once have that might warrant a study? He thought even harder about his high school experience and how he had barely managed to survive, and thought even harder yet about which subject he did the least poor job in.

Clearly, he had taken too long to respond, and so Sheryll interrupted his thoughts. "I see," she said in a toneless voice, putting emphasis on the latter to really indicate the conclusion she had come to. "You and Macie are very different, aren't you?"

***

They had quarrels before, but never one as monstrous as this. He had come home from work late, but she had arrived even later. She had gotten to the point in her college career that she was beginning to think further about the future. It had been a topic of their discussion quite a few times, and the conversation usually ended with him telling her that he would follow her wherever she went and that he would support her in whatever she did. And so, when she came home that night with a smile on her face, he was elated to hear whatever good news she would present.

She grabbed his hands and sat down on the couch. She lightly brushed a tress of auburn hair behind her ear, the strand perfectly blending in alongside the rest of her locks. "I'm so excited," she began, as though the marriage of her dimples and freckles had been a secret to him. She took a shallow breath as if for theatrics more than practicality. "As you know, I've been looking into internships."

123

He nodded. He had spent countless hours with her as she perfected her applications. She had asked him to read through them a couple of times, but he could never find any faults in them. Besides, should they exist, he wasn't sure whether he would be able to identify them.

"Well, I got a call earlier today," she continued. "I got the internship in Wincaster City!" She pulled her smile back to reveal her teeth He could tell that this was something of which she was incredibly gratified. But there was something that didn't quite make sense to him.

"Wincaster City?" he asked her. "I didn't realize there was a Wincaster City near us." He knew that there was the famous Wincaster City, "*Pertinacia et ignis,*" but surely that could not be the one she referred to. There must be a similarly-named town nearby that had won her heart.

"Well," she started. Her smile began to fade, the dimples now hiding away. "There's not. I applied for an internship position at the Wincaster University Hospital, and they say they're really excited to have me! I would start-"

"Hold on a second," he hesitated, his voice emerging a bit more stern than he had anticipated. He paused to consider apologizing but continued anyway. "I thought you said that you weren't applying to anywhere that was more than 50 miles away," he clarified.

"I did but-"

"You couldn't possibly commute! I mean, Wincaster City is… is how far away? It's gotta be somewhere around 200 miles!"

"176," she corrected as though the 24 miles would make all the difference. "But I really think-"

"When did you even fill out this application? Why didn't you tell me about it first? We could've talked about it!"

"We *are* talking about it!" she urged. She looked down and realized that somewhere in their conversation, their hands had departed. "I worked really hard for this, and this is something I really want to do. It's a great opportunity and I really want you to come with me."

"To come with you…"

"Yes. You said you'd follow me anywhere, right?"

He paused. He wanted time to digest- to anticipate. He was feeling overwhelmed with emotions that he couldn't possibly name. He had no desire to name them. "So you're moving?" His voice had become cold and sharp, as though it had aged through his silence, like a fine wine.

"I… I would like to," she responded, matching his energy. "I want you to come with me."

"Where would we get the money?" he asked her.

"What do you mean?"

"What do I mean?" he pressed, his voice intensifying and whirling out of control. "I work minimum wage, weeding gardens, and you spend all your time in class! We barely have enough money to make rent at the end of each month!"

"We can ask my parents."

"Your parents are spending all of their money on Sheryll at Damask. I heard your father talking on the phone the last time they visited. They're having trouble making ends meet, too."

"Why would you say that?" she responded, and the hope that she had been portraying withered away. "Why were you even- I can't *believe* you," she hissed. She pressed her fingertips to her temples. "Can we ask your-"

"You know very well that we can't," he returned.

The room fell silent. They both waited for the other to break the silence, a waiting game that seemed to last an eternity. Every second chipped away at their being more and more. It was just a matter of who would crack first.

"I'll take on another job," he decided. He wanted to ensure he would be able to make whatever dreams she had come true. He wanted to be the one in her life to make everything around her sparkle. He wanted to be the driving force that she carried along with her wherever she went. He wanted to be with her.

"You don't have the time," she responded, breaking him back into reality. He almost felt embarrassed that he had been the one to fall into a trance of unrealistic hopes, now.

"I could make time. I could take on some night shifts somewhere. Maybe I could learn to bartend." He spoke, but he knew that this was not something that was going to happen. He simply continued to speak as if someone had taken control of his body and was trying to drive him further into this argument.

"Listen," she crooned. "I just… I don't know. You work so much already. I'd hate to see you… to see you so stressed out."

"You could take up a job," he responded, probably quicker than she would have liked to hear. He realized it sounded rude and accusatory, and so he allowed the force within him to continue his reasoning. "You have time in between studying. I know you're on campus longer than you need to be."

"Longer than I need to be?" Her voice rose. "I study so damn hard and I come home and keep studying. I'm always either in class, studying, or commuting between the two."

"Well, what about now? You're gonna spend your time arguing with me when you could be working?"

"And what do you mean by that?"

"I'm just saying I work all the time, and you- what? You sit around and read all day. What classes are you even taking?"

"I take the classes I need to take!"

"Well, maybe you wouldn't need to take those classes if you got a little more in-person experience!"

"Well, maybe if you went to college, you would understand where I'm coming from!"

"Well, maybe we're just... very different people!"

Silence flooded the room once again, but this time it was not fought over. The war was already over.

"Well, maybe we are," she concluded, standing up. She grabbed her jacket and started towards the door.

"Where are you going?" he asked her urgently. "Stop! Where are you going?"

But there was no changing her mind. The door slammed, marking a renaissance of silence- one that could only be combated alone. He sat there, allowing it to envelop him. His mind replayed her words over and over. *Well, maybe we are.* The door slams once more, sending a shattering echo through his mind. *Well, maybe we are.* And with every reiteration he experienced, as if for the first time, the hollowing loneliness that crept with it. He longed to have her by his side, and he didn't dare turn his head for the fear that he would be granted reality. Did he win the quarrel? It did not matter to him. There was no winner. Both were left with a feeling of insufficiency.

***

He had never seen so much blood in his life. It flowed like branches of a tree, climbing into whatever wrinkles and canyons her body displayed, the crimson infecting the skin greedily. It was difficult to find the source of the bleeding, but he knew there was definitely a large gash bisecting her neck, and it appeared as though her clothes had been slashed. He didn't even think about what creature could have possibly possessed paws plump enough to house such thick claws- or were they jaws?

Her body was much heavier than he had ever noticed, and it was awkward to drag along, but he kept at it. He thought heavily about how much simpler a task it would have been, should she have survived whatever had struck her, but he knew he wouldn't be in his situation without it. It didn't help that the body was still limp, rigor mortis not yet settling in. He watched as some of the tresses of her auburn hair would catch in the foliage and create a wreath. Part of him longed to see her swipe her fingers across her brow and salvage her once-kept ponytail, only for him to realize her arms would sweep no longer. Oh, what a dilemma he was in. She had been the one to drag him into these woods, and here he was trying to drag her out. And yet he knew what the world around him would see and in which direction the fingers would point, and so he endeavored for the sake of himself.

And so, in that moment, he knew exactly where the body had to go. He recalled the sight of a river in the distance, the slight whooshing signaling that life was nearby, readying its hands to be juxtaposed. He wasn't sure if it was truth or exaggeration, but the terrain appeared to be bubbling under his feet, creating hills and divots to snag her body every chance it could possibly get, pulling her this way and that, very much like how she had done to him throughout their lives together. She had grown to be so commanding and stubborn, and yet here she was being exactly that, and yet the opposite. Perhaps these hills would swarm him and squeeze him until his bones would crush between them like glass, digesting him and soaking up the nutrients.

He would need an alibi, he soon realized. *They'll suspect something if I leave without her,* he thought to himself. At the moment, he wasn't entirely sure who he would be convincing. They had no children, and their parents were all long gone. Perhaps Sheryll would send questions their way, but she could easily be neglected. Besides, he would be able to pass off the death as a silent response to their newly complicated relationship. Conceivably, he could use this as part of his excuse. He pictured himself telling of their terrific fights and how she had stormed off. Perhaps even never to be seen again (not necessarily false in this situation). Yes, it was perfect! But then he thought about what she would have done. Where had she gone? She most likely would have wound up back home sooner or later. How would he account for that? Her belongings were still in their house, and she assuredly would have paperwork and appointments to attend to. He knew that whatever fallacy he told would have to include her demise in some way or another.

Cardiac arrest was the next thought on his mind. His pal back home had passed away from it while the two of them were working on a project together, and so he knew the symptoms and what it would look like. But then he thought about further inquiries and how he *did* have this experience. People might suspect that he would have known what to do in this situation and claim he had left her to die on purpose. Besides, he would be leaving her body behind, and he could not think of an excuse for this may be, other than the weight, of course. Would people expect this of him? He didn't want to have to make the decision, and so he opted for another alibi.

There was always suicide, he knew. But he thought about her and the life she had lived. Would it be believable to the people who knew her? Was it ever something that was believable? No one would ever picture someone in their lives to make an attempt until it happens, and then in those moments, they rewind to all of the warning signs and cries for help they had shaken off when they first appeared. Perhaps if he told people of her "suicide," they would begin to see ignored signs and pick up symbolism like an English class he had barely been able to pass. Suicide, yes, was an option. But it was not one he wanted to use. Something about it felt sour to him, as though it repainted her entire life like a poor art restoration. Yes, he would need something more genuine, and one that even he could believe.

At that moment, his attention turned to the snow. How long had it been falling? Light dustings blew down from the speckles of leaves and rested on his head, their long journeys coming to an end. He hadn't even realized how the temperature had dropped since he had been so caught up in discovering and dragging, and the burden of the exertion had actually caused him to break a sweat. But now the beads of sweat and flakes of snow contradicted each other on his balding scalp, each one trying to convince him in one way or another whether he should stop to dress further or continue on in his endeavors. Perhaps he should tell the inquisitive that she had suffered from hypothermia. Yes, this would be a sufficient explanation. But how long does it take for someone to die from hypothermia? And would they question why he had been the survivor? Would they label him as selfish and ponder why he hadn't done more in his power to protect the woman he claims to love? He decided to put a bookmark in this one and tuck it into the back of his mind. He would use it, should he not be able to produce a better explanation, but for the moment, he was mentally exhausted.

It took another thirty-two minutes for him to reach the river, but to him it felt more like two hours. Yes, two hours of struggling to wiggle the body through bushes and branches, finding concerns when something would snag on her shirt, revealing her stomach, full of slashes and gashes from who knows what creature. Her body had become pretty dirty at this point, some moisture from the ground settling in her skin and staining her clothes. Each bump on the trail left behind something else for her to pick up. They would seep into the wounds, and he felt inclined to brush them off, but he knew that in the end, none of it would matter.

He hadn't realized he had been hearing the river for some time, the white noise of it settling wavelengths in the oxygen he breathed in, but now that he was next to it, he noticed how thunderous the churning of the water was. A part of him felt naked, despite the sounds surrounding him. He feared that whatever had murdered her would so easily be able to sneak up behind him, given the volume of the river. He swore that he could feel the gaze of someone burning into the back of his sweaty neck. And so with that, he made haste and dragged her body further, stepping onto the rocks, each one quivering under his footing. The sound of her body rolling the rocks underneath her added more noise to the cacophonous river, making him more paranoid with each step. He found himself accelerating, wobbling his way into the frigid water despite his aching back and sore legs. There was a job to be done.

He was shivering waist-deep in the river when he decided to let her go. He looked down at her body, which was beginning to be enveloped by the river, each molecule of water clinging onto her skin and pulling her further under like the undead trying to claim her as their own. He noticed the reddening of the water, as they cleansed the wounds in her flesh as if to try to tear away any barriers between them. He now had a clearer view of the damage. It was as though he wasn't looking at a body but rather a dog toy that had been thrown around and well-attacked. He almost imagined white stuffing to emerge from the gashes, but only saw more vermilion. Every part of her body was shredded- her throat, her arms, her legs, her torso. Whatever had attacked her had done so with some sort of weapon. It appeared as though the marks were too thick to have been from an animal's claw. Perhaps a bear, he thought, only to realize he had never seen a bear in person and was entirely uncertain how the size of a bear's claw compared to that of his dead wife's lacerations. But it was then that he realized something that left a nauseating pit in his stomach.

The attacker had ripped her flesh, but spared her face. He knew with this that whatever had left slashes in her body either had a sort of humanity to it, or could not reach her face. Although if it couldn't reach her face, what shape would it have been with its claws? He made the assumption that whatever it was had been human and spared her once-auburn hair and now-dim amber eyes whatever mutilation it had done to the remainder of her body. Observing the specks of blood among her freckles, he used the water around him to cleanse her skin. He looked into her amber eyes for the last time. Their gaze had no focus but rather peered into the heavens. What had been the last thing that they had seen? He thought of a myth she once told him about a woman turning men to stone, petrifying them. The pit in his stomach grew a sour fruit when he wondered what her last moments could have been like. He found himself pleading to whoever could possibly be watching her that she had not died in a state of fear. Something about this caused him to ache. And so he closed her eyes as if they were his own. They didn't open until she had reached the bottom, and with that, he knew the job had been sufficient.

Chapter Ten

You will live with the very trees you strove to protect; I hope they realize this and protect you, their love draping over you like a blanket, and their kisses tickling your eyelashes.

It took Jim quite some time to recover. Although his condition was not severe, it was still enough to scare the duo into cautious habits and practices. Clara eventually learned to better care for her father, and though he was recovering, he would still try his best to care for his daughter. Unlike her mother, Jim would take the time to cook dinner and even continue to work from home, despite his condition. However, he made sure to demonstrate each task to Clara so she could replicate it independently, God forbid she would ever have to.

This would, unfortunately, also mean that Clara would not have as much time to spend with Jessica Heathers. They would see each other in class or around the school, but the class and hallways did not yield much conversation. And so they honored the time they had together after school, in which they would talk about the events of their lives. Clara often would only converse about her father and her classes, and so she felt as though Jessica Heathers would bring more worth to their chats. They would go on long walks, hiking in the woods nearby. This served as a healthy outlet for any hindering emotions while also allowing them their sacred privacy.

There had been an instance in which Jessica Heathers had even invited Clara on a blind double date as she felt as though it would strengthen and solidify their relationship with each other, but also provide stability and flattery for their relationships with the men. Jessica Heathers knew that Clara had never been steady with anyone and took it into her hands to find someone worthy of her friend's love. However, this did not work out well as Jessica Heathers and her date wound up arguing over appetizers, and both Clara and her date were rather introverted and spoke very little to the other. After they left the restaurant, Clara and Jessica Heathers took to their own accounts without their dates.

"Did you see the way he ate with his fingers?" Jessica Heathers asked Clara, gesturing to demonstrate.

"I mean, it *was* finger food."

"But besides that. I mean, chocolate cake? How do you eat cake with your fingers? I've heard of people arguing over whether you eat cake with a fork or a spoon, but *him*? I guess he just came up with his own answer."

"That *was* pretty gross." She thought about it for a second. Typically, she would try to think of a few nice things to say about whoever Jessica Heathers was dating, but ultimately wind up generating everything negative she could possibly calculate. "I just didn't like the way he was talking about that girl's makeup."

"How she looked like a clown?"

"Yeah. Except she didn't. I feel like it's not his business to comment on other people like that. I mean, I could say plenty of things just about his hair, but I'm not going to."

"I guess. But I mean, she could always change her makeup. It's not like he's making fun of her nose or something she's stuck with."

"I don't think people should be making fun of anyone at all," Clara asserted. "Imagine if he was talking about you to all of his friends like that. If he says it about random people like that, it's quite probable."

Jessica Heathers smiled. "You realize you're pointing out things that you don't like about him. How is that different from what he's doing?"

"It's plenty different. For one, I'm configuring everything that defines him as a horrible person. He's delineating beauty standards."

"I suppose you're right." The two continued along their trail, allowing the crumbling sound of stones beneath their feet to fill the empty spaces in their conversation. "There wasn't going to be a second date anyway. It's just nice to know you always have my back." The pebbles beneath their feet continued to crunch. "I take it you're not having a second date either?"

"Some people just don't mix," Clara explained, her eyes drifting from her friend. "Besides, we were too invested in your 'conversation' to have our own."

They reached the peak of the trail, the trees thinning out before them and expanding the land to a clifftop. The two had witnessed this view many times during the day, but never at night. It felt as though they stood among the stars, each one dotting the night sky as though someone flicked a paintbrush to spray them into the sky. Below them were houses and buildings, the lights shining through the windows indicating the life within them. Everything seemed so distant, whether it be the burden of civilization or their own thoughts.

"Life is so unpredictable," Jessica Heathers stated. "You could be fine one day, walking down the street, fine-perfectly fine, and then suddenly a car or a rabid animal or something wild comes out of nowhere, and it's the end for you. Or you could wake up one day and learn you've been in a coma for the past seventeen years and that your husband basically sees you as dead and has remarried and now has three kids that look just like your old English teacher. Or your brain straight up like- disagrees with you and you have a stroke or- or- or something and you have to learn how to live your life normally again. Anything could happen- anything.And there are so many different possibilities- so many different outcomes." Clara looked at her to demonstrate her concerns. The way she spoke was so swift and passionate. She wondered if Jessica Heathers was on the verge of hyperventilation, judging by how she had to gasp for air between words as though she was submerged in water and trying to resurface. "It's so hard to know what choice is the right choice- if there even- if there even is such a thing as a 'right choice.' And even if there is, we can't think ahead far enough because with... with each choice stems another million or so, and there are so many different possibilities. So many. And there's no going back after we make a choice. There's no redo button- we can't. . . We can't go back. Whatever we do, we're just stuck. And then life is over. There's no second chance."

Clara tried to compose a response, but nothing sparked inside her mind. It was just as Jessica Heathers said: there were too many options to choose from.

"Everything is changing. But at the same time, everything stays the same." Jessica Heathers looked to Clara for her insight. She tried to look into her eyes and noticed her pupils quavering as though they were shaking in fear of the unknown. "How is that possible?"

"There are cells in our bodies birthing every moment of the day, but there are also cells dying. After enough time, your body becomes something entirely new, and you'd never know it because it all feels the same. I think it's just about the perspective you take. Whether you look at the minuscule or the grander view," Clara contributed.

Neuroplasticity (noun)— the brain's ability to change and grow in a way that reminds you that the frontal lobe is what makes us human.

Jessica Heathers continued to look ahead. Clara was uncertain whether she had processed what she had told her. "It's scary. You'll never know what someone else is thinking. Something you'd never thought of could just pop up out of the blue, and you'd never be prepared enough because it never crossed your mind." She looked at Clara. "How am I supposed to prepare myself for something if I don't know what it is or when it's coming?"

Clara searched for the correct response. She sorted through the contents of her mind to try to replicate an answer that would be suitable. But then she realized that whatever response she gave would never be sufficient. "You don't," she replied. "You just go about your life and hope for the best," she concluded. "You remain optimistic that whatever approaches you has a purpose and that whatever it may be brings you satisfaction in the long run."

Jessica Heathers stood up, so suddenly that it nearly startled Clara. She edged her way to the edge of the cliff, the wind picking up tresses of her hair and whipping them around her face. She opened her arms, closed her eyes, and leaned her head back.

This alarmed Clara. She found herself on her feet without even thinking about the action, but hesitated. She didn't want to alarm her friend in fear that she would fall, but she was also concerned about the possible recklessness Jessica Heathers might cause. But before she had time to react, Jessica Heathers took a step backwards, Clara's heart now racing. She released her breath in a sigh.

They stood in silence, Clara rushing through scenarios in her mind and how to best respond to them, should she need to. But finally, Jessica Heathers spoke.

"I want to know everything that happens next."

***

Jessica Heathers had not been present in class. Clara had considered that she had possibly been absent due to illness until she received a note in her handwriting instructing her to meet at one of their hiking spots. She had assumed that this would be at the time of day in which they would usually meet, and so she appeared to find Jessica Heathers awaiting her arrival. Her face was hidden as though she was making an effort not to be recognized, and her hands clutched her jacket, her arms folded across her chest. Something told Clara to wait, not necessarily to approach Jessica Heathers but rather to allow her to initiate the conversation herself.

"It's beautiful up here," Jessica Heathers said, the statement somehow acknowledging Clara's presence. "Not the most beautiful place we've seen, but it's... it's..."

"Satisfactory?" Clara offered.

"Yeah," Jessica Heathers agreed. "Satisfactory." The word seemed foreign in her mouth.

Clara grew more concerned the longer she stared at her friend. Although she couldn't see her face too well, she could picture the gloss of tears erupting in her eyes.

"I want us to travel the world together," Jessica Heathers told Clara. "We can go hiking in every corner of the earth and we can explore the places people have been far too afraid to witness themselves," she declared. Her voice accelerated as she spoke. She pulled out a map and pointed to a location with a quivering finger. "We're going to go here one day," she told her. "There's so much culture and mythology surrounding it. So many people have gone in and so few have survived. But I know that we could do it together. We could do anything together. We'll do our research. We'll practice other hikes. We'll work our way up. We can do it. It's on this huge mountain with a forest full of thick trees, and we can search for the river and watch it disappear before our eyes. Can you imagine that? The water evaporates because it gets so hot during the day, but then it freezes over at night. Apparently, there are some legends that it's not even real water. Wouldn't that be neat to see? And when it is night, we can find the ravine and watch the snow drift through the treetops. Imagine that! It's been said that it's the most beautiful spot! I know we would be able to do it."

"Of course!" Clara responded, stunned at the urgency Jessica Heathers was presenting. "When will we embark?"

"Whenever we can get away from this place," she told her, making it clear that she had thought this through in detail. "When we're ready to go on our own, whenever that may be. Obviously, we can't go right now because there's so much to learn about it and so much equipment that we need, but one day, one day we're going to make it there. Even if we wind up drifting apart, we'll reunite one day and see the world. We can start looking into it today-right now-if we want!"

Clara was elated to hear this, but she felt skeptical. Why had this come up so suddenly? "Is everything alright?" she asked her friend. She wanted to see why she was hiding her face, but knew she had to stay in line.

Jessica Heathers turned away. "What do you think happens to us when we die?"

"Is everything alright?" Clara reiterated. "Jessica Heathers, you know you can tell me anything."

"I like to think there's a bright light- something warm and welcoming. I know that's really cliche, but I'd like to think of death as something to acknowledge- something you shouldn't fear."

"Jessica," she tried to calm her, but to no avail.

"What do you think?"

She paused before answering the question. "One moment you're there, the next you're not. No bright light or anything. It happens quickly, so you have no time to be afraid. A bright light just doesn't make sense to me."

"Clara," Jessica Heathers began. She allowed the name to float into the air, gliding in the wind and eventually dissolving into nothing like the last upbow of a symphony. She uncovered her face, revealing splotches of black and purple across her face.

"What happened?" she demanded.

"It was my fault," she argued in return.

"Who did this to you?" She looked into her sunken eyes and knew right away. "I thought you weren't seeing him anymore. I thought you guys disagreed."

"He's got some really great qualities, I promise. We just weren't seeing eye-to-eye."

"So, he hit you?"

"It was my fault," she repeated. "We were just arguing and then…"

"This is not your fault," Clara assured. "We have to go to the police. He can't be doing this to you. We can't let him-"

"We can't," she responded in a flat voice.

"Of course we can. We just go to them and tell them that your ex-"

"He's not my ex," Jessica Heathers interjected.

"That someone you went on a date with-"

"We're still together," Jessica Heathers concluded. Clara stared at her, processing the words but not allowing them to digest properly. "Look, it was just a one-time thing. It's not going to happen again." She looked away. "I just… I just needed someone to talk to about it." Clara felt as though language was disintegrating before her eyes. "Next time, I won't get in the way, and next time, I won't anger him this much. It… It was my fault," she reiterated in an attempt to convince.

"Jessica," Clara started, still scurrying to find the right words. "You deserve so much better than him," she explained. "You deserve someone who will love you as you are- someone who won't overwhelm you with consequences.

Love should be easy, especially for someone like you. I guess what I'm saying is that you deserve someone equally as wonderful as you- someone with grace and beauty and intelligence and kindness."

"Clara," she began, looking away.

She looked into her eyes, the tears allowing them to sparkle in the most bittersweet way. The warm green over her eyes seemed to turn them to emeralds. But as Clara's eyes focused on the rest of her face and the splotches of black and purple, she felt herself overwhelmed with a feeling she had been feeling all along but was never magnified to this extent until this very moment.

And so Clara leaned forward, pressing her lips against her friend's, something she had wanted to do for a very long time that she had never had the courage to execute. She placed her right hand on her cheek and used her left to pull her closer. She could smell just how sweet she was. She felt how soft her skin was underneath her palms. The wind, like music, accompanied the echo of Jessica Heather's voice, intertwining itself through their hair, allowing silky, straight fringes to appear where coiled locks ended. The world around her began to melt away as though it had all been a painful hallucination that would now be replaced with the reality of nirvana. She was in absolute bliss.

But Jessica Heathers pushed her away. "Clara," she said, the tone in her voice indicating rejection. "I'm so sorry." She stood up. "I can't. I should go. I should tell- I should go." She began rushing away, wiping her lips with the back of her hand.

"Jessica Heathers!" she called after her friend. "Jessica!" But nothing stopped her.

She felt something awaken in the pit of her stomach. Was it longing? Anger? Jealousy? Guilt? She couldn't name it. All that she knew was that this was the end of something that would never begin.

***

Jessica Heathers refused to speak to her after the incident. She grew quieter in school, and Clara couldn't tell if she was withdrawing because of the kiss or her boyfriend's abuse. She was devastated every time she would be around town, whether picking up groceries or going on walks to replace the hikes she and Jessica Heathers used to take, and she would see the very same girl with the boy who had beaten her. He would drag her around from place to place, and her head was always hung low. Even if Clara had been able to capture her gaze, she was uncertain whether she would return a smile. He would catch Clara staring, however. And every time he would guide Jessica Heathers in front of him and express through his face that he knew exactly what happened that one day.

Clara considered approaching the boy and trying to talk some sense into him. Unfortunately, Jessica Heathers was always glued to his side. If she were to speak to him, she would have to withstand the two of them together, and she knew that she would not be able to address her friend. Her other option was to await the end of their relationship. Jessica Heathers never stayed with the same man for too long. However, for some reason, it seemed as though this relationship was lasting much longer than the others. She would awaken every morning with the hope that she would catch one of them alone and know that their demise had been met, but she failed to see the day.

Jessica Heathers' bruises would migrate around her face and body, sometimes swelling and other times fading to a yellowish tint. On her walk home from school, she would pass the police station, and every day, something compelled her to stop and wonder what conversations could have been held. But then Jessica Heather's voice would interject in her head, and Clara would continue on, trying her hardest not to turn back. The bruises would continue to pop up like mosquito bites, each one staining her face one day and slowly dying away as though it were a blossoming flower- a weed, perhaps. It pained Clara to see her every day, and so she spent as much time inside with her father as she could, only traveling into the town when completely necessary.

***

The snow gradually turned to rain as she sat in the tent she had set up. She listened as it would pitter on the slush- a mixture of the past and present in precipitation- and felt satisfied that she had packed so many extra socks. Her eyes gazed into the map she had brought, but she couldn't find herself concentrating on the shapes and figures held within it. She wondered to herself what her journey would be like had Jessica Heathers been with her, but she forbade herself from the thoughts. Still yet, they grew back like an ever-growing plague, infecting every inch of her mind. She ached to know what a conversation with Jessica Heathers would be like after all of these years- years of silence and allowing hindrance to turn into regrets. She observed the precipitation from the slight comfort of her tent, and she imagined her life sparkling in one raindrop and Jessica Heathers in the next. Were they going to intersect once and then descend to never meet again, or would they become part of the same puddle, providing nutrients and life to the surrounding plants?

But her thoughts were interrupted by the slightly familiar trudging (and now splatting) sound arising from the distance. A part of her had hoped that it would be the beautiful Jessica Heathers, somehow knowing that she would be coming to the woods and deciding to embark on her own journey in search of her and mending their mangled, perplexed relationship. However, Clara knew that this would not be the case and that she had to remain level-headed, especially in a land such as this where ice turns to water and then evaporates before the naked eye.

She was interrupted once more by the introduction of a figure. She had only seen the man once before, but the shape of the figure combined with the horrible sloshing of the melting snow informed her that this was the same person. Something was a little different about him this time. He seemed fatigued and full of worry, unlike the overwhelming confidence he had demonstrated for her the first time.

"Hey!" he called, seemingly excited to grace her presence once again. The tempo of his sloshing feet accelerated.

Perhaps she could have closed herself in the tent, but she knew that she would only corner herself. She considered walking away, but had the impression that he would amble along until she acknowledged herself. And so, she decided to do what she did best: respond skeptically.

"What do you want?" she asked him, emphasizing her tone and articulating the consonants in an attempt to demonstrate her neglect to answer.

"Boy, am I happy to see you!"

How forward, she thought to herself. *I barely know the man, and he acts like it's been years since we've seen each other*. Still, she took note of how bright his face seemed to glow despite the worry and fatigue pulling at the wrinkles in his brow.

"I thought I told you to leave me alone," she responded, trying to stand up tall for the man who was now relatively close.

Doug realized at this moment that he could tell Clara what had happened. Yes, he still hadn't figured out an alibi. But it was very likely that she would understand, given the circumstances they were in. These woods clearly were preyed upon by something voracious, and he wanted to ensure her safety as well as his own.

"Clara, we're in danger," he told her. "We have to leave right away!"

"Danger?" she repeated. "Maybe from the severe weather and the occasional steep incline, but that's all. Unless you're trying to tell me you have something planned," she accused.

"There's something in the woods."

Clara scoffed. "There's nothing in the woods except trees. The conditions aren't vital. People have barely come out alive, let alone animals." She looked him up and down. "Unless *you're* having a problem with people approaching you out of nowhere and bugging you, too."

"You're wrong," Doug told her. "Something is in the woods and it's- it's dangerous! You have to believe me!"

"And how did you manage to escape this 'dangerous' creature?"

"I didn't!" he exclaimed. "It took my wife, Macie! I found her body. I can't even begin to describe- It had to be the workings of something truly ferocious!"

"Your *wife*?" Clara repeated. "You have a wife, and yet you had the audacity to approach me and flirt?"

"That's- that's not what I want you to take away from this," he defended.

"How am I supposed to believe you? You're unfaithful to your wife, and then you come here and expect me to believe you when you tell me these woods are dangerous, and that I'm in danger when the only thing threatening me is *you*!"

"Macie— no. Clara! Please. We have to get out of here."

"I have an expedition," she told him. "And I plan to finish it." She narrowed her eyes. "Alone."

"Please, I'm begging you to listen to me."

"*God*, don't you hear me?" she cried. "No means no! Clearly, you don't understand how these things work, but when a girl expresses her disinterest, you leave her *alone*. You don't keep- keep *forcing* yourself on her until she feels desperate enough to settle for someone as grotesque as *you*! Like sometimes no matter what you do, someone's just— they're just not going to like you!"

This finally helped Doug realize that he would not be able to convince her. "Fine," he accepted. "I'll be on my way then. But don't say that I didn't warn you." He took a few steps past her. "And by the way, that's not how you're supposed to react when a man tells you his wife is dead."

She watched as he disappeared into the woods, uncertain what she should file as the truth. Did he actually have a wife?

She thought back to her thorough research of these woods and how the few survivors had returned mentally ill, most likely from fatigue or dehydration. Still, none of the survivors yielded any information about creatures lurking. Those who didn't survive would rather have been lost to the hostile environment. Clearly, Doug would be lost as well, whether physically or mentally. She believed it to be the latter.

***

She was just about finished packing up her tent. She was hoping to make some good distance before the sun reached its peak and it became too torrid for comfortable travel. She would continue to travel, but would stay close to the stream to avoid losing it entirely, especially when it would disappear at the peak of the day. It had been so difficult for her to find level ground in the woods for her to set up, so while she began to trudge through the jarring earth, she found herself hoping she would be lucky enough to find another campsite later on. She filtered some water from the stream- hopefully enough to last her until dusk. She brought it to her lips only to notice an odd bitter taste to it. Unguarded, she gasped, taking in particles of the mysterious liquid and choking on it. She coughed until she felt a rattle in her throat and wiped her mouth. Might as well get started on her hike for the day.

As she lumbered through the woods, she took note of the shapes of the trees around her, partially for recognition purposes, but mostly for the sake of enjoying the scenery. She saw some trees that were incredibly vast, causing her to wonder what their lives would have been like centuries ago when they had first been naught but saplings. Other trees were quite thin, beginning their own journeys through the woods. She stumbled across an array of bushes painted with a variety of colors, exciting her to think of how precise her timing must have been to witness them in full bloom. She thought of how beautiful they would look in a bouquet on her kitchen counter, but left them as they were. It was not her place to alter their destinies.

But the orange flowers caught her most off guard. She wanted to sniff them and fill her brain with the scent of oranges, allowing her to reminisce about her mother. Part of her understood that the flowers most likely would not smell of oranges, but she liked to believe in her mind that they would send her mind into a state of nostalgia. They were so beautiful and she imagined herself lying in them and letting the petals tickle her skin with the aid of the breeze, and maybe— just maybe— it would feel like eyelashes and a gentle breath of someone who meant something to her. She did not want to take the chance of being disappointed, and so she left them alone.

And then she heard a voice, soft and melodious like a song she had heard before. At first, she couldn't quite make out its vocabulary, but after it slowly crescendoed, she realized that it was unmistakably calling her name.

"Clara," it teased, presenting itself as a female voice. Its timbre was familiar. She knew exactly to whom it belonged. "Clara, I've missed you," she sang.

She found herself scrambling for words. She had hoped for this encounter far more than she could possibly put into numbers. Should she apologize? Part of her considered turning towards the voice and simply running, but she knew such a gesture would be far overdramatic. But Clara realized that an overwhelming sensation of shame was washing over her. It had been years- how many? It's been over ten. People change, especially over such a span. Why hadn't she apologized earlier? What would have happened in such an encounter? She then thought of her justification for refusing to provide help to her friend's relationship.

This was a moment that she chose to withdraw from. And so, Clara simply responded, "I apologize, but I must be on my way," and turned onto her trail.

She listened as the voice continued to call after her, but pretended as though it never existed in the first place.

Pachun Research Laboratories
Incorporated

Dear Mr. Howard Lewis,

First of all, we would like to thank you for your interest in Pachun. We have received your application and were impressed by your previous research and work. We are pleased to offer you a position as one of our Head Researchers on our team entitled, The **Cure**. Your starting salary would be $78,000, should you accept. We would like your response by the 30th of this month.

Upon accepting, we will send you all of the necessary paperwork associated with onboarding, along with any physicals and drug tests required by the corporation. You should be fit to have your first day following 5-7 business days after our recipient of these documents.

We thank you again for your interest and look forward to working with you in the future. We truly believe you would be an exceptional addition to our team.

Sincerely,

Dr. James Grieg

Hiring Manager

Pachun Research Laboratories Incorporated

1236 Stork Street, 207B

Chapter Eleven

It's a quiet night- your favorite type- and I swear I sense your perfume amid the breeze tangling its fingers through my hair.

The core of humanity buds from imperfection, and with it come branches and branches of moments otherwise labelled to be regrettable or embarrassing. Humans learn to grow through the constant inner dialogue of "is this right? Is this wrong?" and having to delicately balance all of the gray areas into respective niches. And even more, they spend so much time attempting to categorize and refusing to admit to the ambiguity of it all that they teach themselves to feign perfection and decline their errors. With this, oftentimes, they come to quarrel with one another since they never want to submit to the truth and think so highly of their own rapport that they never consider the bleeding impact their actions truly have. And so they spend their lives seeking **cures** and answers to rhetoric that yield answers only satisfactory to mankind as opposed to embracing the dubiety life was intended to be.

This introduces the scientist. It is possible for a man to be a scientist and philosopher. But the fact that science lies in fact and philosophy in ambiguity, this particular man never learned to love the two, picking the one child he favors more and leaving the other to the unfamiliar confines of nature. He invested his life into science, disregarding the naysayers and nonbelievers. He would read book after book in attempts to grasp and grapple with any bits of information he did not otherwise know and to confirm the information that was familiar to him. And he hoped that one day he would be able to assist in the discovery of any information that books failed to provide him. Logically, this scientist became a researcher.

With a freshly pressed PhD ready to hang on his wall, he spent the first eleven years studying the evolution of *Planaria torva*. He became engrossed in their abilities to regenerate so perfectly from the most severe bisections. Sometimes they would even commence the detachment themselves, the scientist arriving in the lab the next day to find himself a plethora of planaria parts in the petri dishes. There was an instance he was quite proud of in which he was able to grant one lucky (or unlucky) fellow a second head. This mesmerized him greatly. How could such a simple creature hold such a complex ability and present it so flawlessly? He was absolutely engrossed by these adaptations and knew that he would have to study them further and even consider the proper applications of this knowledge.

But after those eleven years, he decided it was time for him to advance. He wanted something more tangible than a flatworm in a dish in his lab. And so he packed up and said farewell and decided to travel, eventually landing himself a job as a researcher of reptiles, the two that intrigued him the most being the *Anolis carolinensis* and the *Chamaeleo chamaeleon,* or the green anole and chameleon, respectively. He was incredibly fascinated by the green anole's ability to camouflage with its surroundings, much like the chameleon, but more so, he was interested in the green anole's tail regenerative properties. He would cut off tails day in and day out just to test and observe and identify until he was ready to rinse and repeat. With the chameleons, he was particularly observant of their abilities to blend in with their surroundings, creating the most vibrant of colors for a variety of reasons. He spent countless hours noting the ever-changing nature of their cells- (chromatophore (noun)— the magician's wand allowing its captors to disappear into thin air and cause its audience to wonder whether it existed in the first place)- and what they endured in order to depict art in the scraggly skin of reptiles.

He had spent another eight years with the reptiles before he was offered a position researching the **Cure**. Pachun Research Laboratories Incorporated was greedy over this **Cure**. Some would call them crazy to pursue such a **Cure**, but the researchers on its case became entranced by its beauty like a pheromone. It became an obsession, but to the public eye, it was simply seen as passion, and passion did he have. Ambition (and perhaps overambition) was something well-known to Pachun, and he was not the type to withdraw from a challenge. And so he packed up his belongings once more and sought out a permanent home so he could dedicate the rest of his life to this project. He was to be working with some of the top scientists- environmentalists, behaviorists, and, of course, other evolutionary biologists. The lab would be much larger than the ones he had previously worked in, at least twice the size. And of course, since the company was much more reputable, he would be receiving much better pay. Simply put, it was the offer of a lifetime, and he accepted it without a second thought.

Nothing would get in his way- except perhaps a vehicle. Blinded by his excitement, as he pulled into the parking lot of the facility, he thought it would be best to back into his parking spot. Now, mistakes do happen, and it is important to note that many of these mistakes happen for good reason. As he backed into another car, he didn't think about how this mistake would change the rest of his life or that any positive consequences would arise from it at all. Instead, he thought of car insurance and writing notes, and possibly even court appearances. He thought of worst-case scenarios of who might be sitting behind the other wheel: his boss? Perhaps a CEO? Dare he peek at the make and model of the car to calculate its worth and apply that to the endless possibilities of ownership? How would he even approach this situation? Does he find the secretary and describe the car to her so she is able to identify its owner? What if, during that process, they appear and see the damage and assume it was a hit-and-run?

But instead, he received a gentle rap on the window and turned to see a woman standing just outside the driver's side. She wasn't the happiest, clearly, but she wasn't as angry as he would have expected. He opened the door and put his hand on his chest.

"I am so incredibly sorry, ma'am. I really didn't mean any harm."

"Accidents happen," she responded. "But um… please move your car so I can assess the damage?"

He felt his face burn. He was so focused on what had just happened that he didn't even bother to pull up or even move his car out of the way.

"I-I'm so sorry! Hold on!" He hopped into his car, straightened it out, feeling the connection of metal unhook. He aligned in the space he had originally intended on claiming, pulled the key out of the ignition, and stepped out of his car, starting towards the woman's bumper. "I'm so sorry, ma'am. Is everything looking alright? I promise I'll pay for any damages!"

She looked up and down at the minor scratch, her arms folded. He thought about her disapproval and what a horrible first impression this must be, whoever she was. He thought about how much he would have to pay for any fixes to be made to restore the car to its former glory. Would this go on the insurance? He expected an array of different reactions from her, but what he was not expecting was this:

"It's just a scratch. You can make it up to me over dinner." She spoke in a flat voice. He couldn't entirely tell if she was joking or not, especially considering how blank her expression was. "That is, if you're not already seeing someone." His heart skipped a beat as though it was trying to rewind her statement. He felt something within him begin to shake. This couldn't be happening. What kind of woman asks out the man who had run into her car? The answer, he discovered, was a fiery woman. She was the type of woman to stamp her identity onto the world and never look back. She was a migrant butterfly on the first day of comfortable temperatures in the year. She was teeth on another's lips, not brisk enough to cause pain, but rather a reaction one had never anticipated they would experience. She was a woman whom he knew he would want.

She burst into laughter, each giggle surfacing from her throat like psychedelic bubbles reaching eagerly for the mesosphere. She smiled and he was delighted to see a gap between her front teeth, almost a reminder of how perfect imperfection is, a relief that this mysterious woman before him is, after all, something tangible.

"Should I take that as a no, or what?" she asked him, looking him in the eyes with a newfound warmness.

"I'd- I'd love to," he responded, surprised to hear words come out of his mouth that he hadn't thought of prior. "I'll pick you up tonight? After work?"

"So long as picking me up doesn't entail hitting my car again," she playfully retorted, throwing in a wink and then turning towards the building and heading in. The moment would have ended there as though it were in a fairytale if it weren't for the fact that they were both heading in the same direction. He contemplated whether he should give her a few moments before he was on his own way, but then realized he would be forgetting his equipment in his car. Absolutely flabbergasted by this woman, he forced himself to calm down with a gulp of air and then tended to his belongings.

***

He was not anticipating that he would find himself out to dinner on this night, and so he felt as though he was not appropriately dressed. Of course, he had dressed professionally for his job, but after spending time in a lab with clothes covering every inch of skin, he found stains on his shirt, accentuated by the contrast of light and dark blue splotches on his dress shirt. He made a mental note to refrain from raising his arms too high to conceal the sweaty mess spreading with nervousness under his arms. Had he been this nervous for his last date? It had been with an older woman he met at the car wash, who immediately opened up to him about her urgency to get married and have children. There was an obvious uncertainty about this relationship that did not yield a second date. The same was not to be said with this woman.

She was also working as a researcher for the same corporation. Unlike him, she was an environmentalist. They were coincidentally both tasked with researching the **Cure**, and they were equally ambitious about finding it, unaware that they were beginning to be swallowed by its tempting grasp. They thought the date ended there. They suspected they had run out of conversation and common ground between them. However, when it comes to connections with others, there is actually much deeper down when you delve into what causes you to differ, and learn how to embrace it. This is what she was the master of, socially. She had unmatched confidence in herself. Beneath it was a sprinkle of awkwardness, but she was able to conceal it so gracefully that you could only wish to see deeper into her skin.

"What do you think of when you fall asleep at night?" she inquired as though the question fell from the sky and landed on the table before them.

"What do you mean?"

"What do you think of to help yourself fall asleep?" she reiterated. "You must think of something. I doubt you fall asleep the second your head hits the pillow.

"I'm sorry, I'm not sure I understand," he responded, investing his thoughts into this question. He was certain that he *did* fall asleep the second his head hit the pillow. He had so much to think about that when it was finally time to rest, he would.

"Think harder," she urged. "What do you think of that immediately calms you down? What's the sign that it's time to turn in for the day? What lives do you replay?"

He looked into her eyes and saw them glisten with curiosity and knew that this was the reason for her being an exceptional scientist. Her constant hunger for excellence and knowledge could only be matched by his own. And he knew that part of that knowledge she longed for resided in him. With this he knew to answer the question. "I think of bread," he responded, realizing how out-of-place it sounded as it traveled from his lips. He started to elaborate. "I used to live across the street from a bakery. If I ever needed a break, I would watch the baker as he made the dough or kneaded it or shaped it. I would watch it rise as it proofed and brown as it baked. On warmer days I'd sit with my back against the house and I could smell the yeast. Sometimes at night I would smell it then too. That's what carries me to sleep."

"How fascinating," she responded, looking into his eyes with an even deeper curiosity. "I can only imagine how soothing that must be."

"What about you?" he returned. "What do you think of?"

She giggled. "I picture myself as an astronaut," she explained.

"Have you always wanted to be an astronaut?"

"I don't even want to be an astronaut now," she replied. He felt his mind now whirling through the conversation again as though he had missed something. "I think of it though. I wonder what it must be like. I can only imagine an incomprehensible silence beyond the machinery and the vastness opened before me ready to swallow me whole- not to consume me but so I can become a part of it and find peace. I picture it in my head to make up for the fact that I would never become an astronaut, nor would I ever *want* to be one."

"I apologize but I don't quite understand," he told her. He thought through her words and even pictured in his mind what she would look like in a spacesuit.

"You can be anything you want to be in your head. If you're imagining it, you know? So why not try to be something you're not? You could see all of the possibilities of the worlds you've never been in."

"The worlds I've never been in?" he echoed, not even noticing his body leaning forward.

"You're familiar with the Multiverse Theory, yes?"

"That there is an endless amount of universes for every possibility, yeah?"

"Exactly. And every single time you picture something that isn't true in this universe, there's another universe where it is the truth." She smirked, the gleam in her eyes indicating that this was only the start of her fantastic madness. "And so, by me imagining I'm in another universe- one that in theory exists- who's to say I'm not technically leaping into another consciousness and seeing through her eyes?"

"Well, I suppose-"

"There's no way to prove it, but there's no way to disprove it. And I choose to be an optimist and declare that I am right."

There were a million responses in his mind, each one shooting through his skull and exploding into different conversations on impact. There was so much to say and so little time to say it, but he replayed her words in his mind and simply smiled. "So you travel to different universes to fall asleep?"

***

They continued to see each other, often falling into the same routine of exploring the vast expanses of each other's mind. This was usually fueled by her ambition to discuss topics he had never thought of, but he found himself asking her more questions as they became more comfortable with each other. He found himself thinking of what questions to ask and even writing them down to avoid forgetting them when they had time to exchange inquiries. On some nights they would talk over dinner and allow the night to take them wherever their hearts deemed fitting, exploring the world around them as though they had never seen it before. Other nights, they would escape and watch the stars as if somehow, they could capture them gliding across the sky as the night cranked its gears. He wasn't sure what a soulmate felt like, but he was certain it was something like this.

Their cooperation only strengthened their work together in the lab. They would be able to exchange data with each other to help find the **Cure**, and the thought of being able to see the other only made them more determined to carry on in their efficiency so that they were able to pass along more information and bear good news to each other. They were given relatively free reign over their studies and so they eventually decided to work together.

There was something about them that made them an exceptional pair and everyone- not just them- was certain that they were going to be the ones to find the **Cure**.

And then one day, he was certain that they had found it. His calculations and investigations had given him an understanding like wiping off spectacles and seeing the world clearly for the first time in- who knows how long? But disagreement began to brew, and the two found a conflict of interest between them.

"You're not going to test it on animals," she told him, rather than asking. "It's inhumane!"

"What would you prefer I do?" he responded. "We have to start from somewhere and by starting with smaller life forms, we'll be able to work our way up to humans and maybe even **cure** this thing!"

"Smaller life forms do not mean smaller-*valued* life forms," she argued. "We're all on this planet for a reason and testing on these animals is going to rob them of their reason!"

"What if their reason is to help give us a **cure**? What if their reason is in the name of science and knowledge and the power that comes with it?"

"I can't believe how incredibly selfish you are!" She turned her head away and took a deep breath. "These animals weren't dropped onto the earth for the sake of helping humans. In fact, I would argue that *humans* were dropped onto Earth for the sake of helping *animals*. And so far, we've done nothing but fail them in the process. Have you seen the way we've torn the Earth apart? All of the irreversible damage that we caused?"

"And that's why we need a **cure**!" He slammed his fist down on the desk. He hadn't even realized how much he had tensed up, let alone realized he was throwing his fist down, until he felt the impact run up his arm. Silence proceeded. He tried to look into her eyes, but she wouldn't turn towards him. His heart sank with regret. "Listen, I'm sorry," he confessed. "I didn't mean for this to get so out of hand. I just-I just don't know what you want me to do here."

A sudden burst of lightness flooded her face. She shifted her arms so they were no longer crossed, but rather clinging to the opposite forearm. Her gaze met his. "Try it on me."

She became progressively sick silently, like cyanide in a peach, something rotten and despicable hidden in something so sweet. Her hair eventually thinned out, resulting in the adorning of head wraps and bonnets to conceal it. She never cared much for wigs since she felt like it would create an inauthentic version of herself, and he chose to respect this. Without her hair, her eyes were accentuated, and he chose to love her even more. That is not to say he had a preference for her with or without hair, but rather that he understood the given circumstances and loved her as if she were two different women, both equally ambitious and strong, but for different reasons.

He continued to take her out at night, just as they normally would, but she found herself fatigued more and more as time went by. Sometimes this would end their evenings early, only allowing them to get a couple of blocks away from the restaurants, but other nights when they opted to stargaze, he would simply bring plenty of thick blankets and quilts and a few pillows and allow her to be lulled into slumber as they watched the stars drift together. Every time she would swear to herself that she would stay awake long enough to watch him nod off for once, but she was never able to.

This, however, did not impede their conversations. He would ask her a million questions if he could, and part of him felt inclined to, as if to compress a lifetime of conversations into a single night. Each response demonstrated a genuine optimism that he could never match. It was as though he was opening a room to discover thousands upon thousands of doors and had the honor of picking and choosing which one he would explore every night.

"So, you wanted to tell me about aliens?" he asked her one night.

"Well, it's not my theory, but I believe in it strongly," she began. "Imagine this: in the future, humans are confined to their homes for hundreds or thousands of years for reasons we don't quite understand at this moment. Their eyes have to change due to a lack of sunlight and the increase in technology. They become bigger and darker. Our skin grays, once again, because we're not subjected to the sun. We've been evolving larger frontal lobes for thousands of years, and we can only assume that they continue to grow: big head. We have all of the knowledge that past generations would have yearned for. And we want to make sure history goes the 'right way.' We want to avoid our mistakes, but in a carefully calculated manner to ensure we get the best possible outcome."

"So, you're saying-"

"I'm saying aliens are humans from the future trying to set things right in the world. There are so many theories about aliens and ancient history- the Great Pyramids and Stonehenge, and countless ancient civilizations. How did they learn all of that on their own? How did humans manage to deviate so much from the other species on this planet? What makes us so special? Well, we have help and inspiration from whom but ourselves!"

"Then what's with all of the probing and abducting?"

"Well, *why* are they confined to their homes? My guess is something happened- maybe an epidemic or something- and they want to provide humans of the past with the antibodies they need in order to fight it off. They want to prolong the human race. What human body first originally developed the ability to fight off diseases?"

"Well, that could've just been evolution and mutation. What if the aliens are just trying to capture research data for them to gain a better understanding of how it affects them in the future? There are so many things we will never understand about the past-maybe the solution is to actually travel to the past and get that data yourself."

"That's true, that's true," she nodded.

"But we also don't know which time travel theory is the most accurate. So would these aliens be from our own dimension or from another? Does everything fall into place as intended or are timelines tampered with?"

"You've got me beat," she smiled.

Silence overtook the conversation, filled with the white noise of spring peepers in a nearby wood. He imagined that she was perhaps spending this time to try to formulate her own response to the question, only to be surprised.

"What do you believe happens to us after death?" This question was different. He could hear a quaver in her voice.

This time he was uncertain how to respond. He had heard the coughs rattling in her throat crescendo and the shudder of her limbs broaden. He replayed her question, the final word hammering into his heart like a creature trying to crawl to safety. "I- I want to hear your theory first," he stated, trying his best to keep his voice still.

She did not hesitate. "Time is an illusion. Our bodies may die, but our conscience lives on. We simply travel back to the beginning and do it all again. But better this time. That's what we see in our dreams, yes? We see the familiarities of other lives and how we can best learn from them and use that to better ourselves the next time around. We are human, after all, and so we have the honor of experiencing change."

"Then I thank the stars," he would tell her, "That they allowed me to spend an eternity with you. And if it only gets better from here, I can only imagine what beautiful things you'll bring to my life the next time around."

"Until the final iteration," she corrected, almost as though he had a complete understanding of the theories she was planting in the wrinkles in his brain.

"The final iteration?"

"When everything is perfect and goes exactly how it's meant to. Finding each other, finding the **Cure**, growing old together- that's the final iteration. And then after that- after that will be the final death."

"How will we know it's final? What's our best-case scenario?"

"The moon," she whispered as though it was a secret to be kept from the stars above them. "In the final iteration, after I'm gone, we'll meet on the moon." She nodded, indicating to him that this had been the first time she had pictured this detail on her own. She confirmed it. "When I-when I leave this world, we'll meet on the moon."

***

"Tell me what you're afraid of!" Howard shrieked at them. His voice had grown hoarse and aggravated after all these years. Had it been from his loss and the failure to meet promises, anticipating the day they would expire? Or had it been from the poison that intoxicated his body day in and day out to provide him with the punishment he felt he deserved for the horrors he brought into his own life, but even worse, *her* life?

"Kill me, already!" His voice growled now as if to imitate them. "I know you have it in you, so why don't you just do it?" He felt his voice begin to break. It wasn't quite snowing yet, but the sky precipitated icy droplets, stinging his face as though daggers fell from the heavens. He looked up to the sky and saw the slanted obliques of the raindrops as they angled themselves towards the ground, never minding the man that stood in their way. They would strike him and tear him down with their crooked fingers if they needed to. They were not afraid, but neither was he.

The branches of the trees obscured his view of the stars. He wished that he would at least be able to see the moon peering down at him like an angel from the heavens, but the leaves were much too thick to allow him satisfaction. He felt as though the trees were huddling around him. Was it comfort or was it antagonizing? He was uncertain, but a part of him didn't care. They could suffocate him for all he cared, and he would only see himself one life closer to hers.

"Why?" he cried to them. "Why aren't you doing it? You *cowards*!" He sobbed, each vocalization rising from his chest like a hiccup. "Is it because I created you? Is that it?" He released a broken sound, allowing all tension within his body to release itself. Had something possessed him? No. It was what he brought unto himself.

He fell to his knees. The moss lining the forest floor soaked like sponges and bled into his trousers. He continued to sob, hardly catching his breath. He finally built himself back up again to weep one final lament. "Just kill me already!"

His face met his hands, the frigid rain no longer restrained. It came down in sheets, plodding onto the back of his head as he hoped something would claim his life. But the world would not give him the same satisfaction he may have found on the moon.

Chapter Twelve

I never imagined we would part in this way and I can't help blaming myself in exactly the manner you would have aspired against

He pinched his wrist, knowing this had all been his fault. He also knew that these people were supposed to be helping them, lifting them out of the situation they had been born into, but now that it was happening, he denied it. He watched as his sister was ushered away from him by a social worker, leading her to whatever house would welcome her- if they would even be welcoming. He was hoping the two of them would be able to stay together, at least after the process sorted everything out, but he doubted this would be the case. He had learned the pain of remaining optimistic. He had heard so many horror stories of foster care and the families that invested in it specifically for the monetary gains and cared very little about the foster children they were actually receiving.

They were going to send him to his uncle. He had heard stories of them separating the children, but a part of him held onto the chance that they would possibly be kept together. He wasn't sure how his sister would be on her own. Would she miss him at night? If the foster family mistreated her, would she know how to defend herself? Would she remember to pack an extra pack of cookies to school because Timmy Jefferson would steal the first? Most of all, he wanted to know if she would be safe, whether it be from her new family, the other kids at school, or from their father. He was supposed to be sent to prison, but what if he escaped somehow? There have been plenty of stories in which prisoners escape, and he knew how inventive and manipulative his father had been.

Was this for the best? He kept replaying the scene in his mind as though his memory was broken and forcing him to submit to the rays of light shining through the window, or the horrid sound, or the distressed tears on his sister's face when he walked in on their father on top of her. He pinched his wrist to try to ground himself back into reality. Sometimes he would pinch too hard and leave a mark that he hoped the counselors at school wouldn't notice. Sometimes they would fade away in time, but sometimes the scene would continue to replay, the radiant lights burning themselves into his eyes to the point where he saw the shape of them when he closed his eyes. The sound would echo as though it was surfacing from all around him, and his sister's face was trying so hard to pry free from their father's hands.

He wasn't entirely certain how long he would be staying at his uncle's house. He knew he had a temper inherited from his father (and his father's from *his* father) on top of a gambling addiction. It would be a few years before he was a legal adult and able to head out on his own. Yes, he'd have to find a job that would take him and find a place to stay, but he would think forward to a summer day, perhaps one a bit too hot for his preference, but he wouldn't care. He would come home from a long day at work, wherever he was, and prepare a nice home-cooked meal for himself and his sister. They would eat it outside on the porch, trying to consume it before the bugs became too attracted to it, and simply enjoy the weather as it cooled with the setting sun. Yes, this is the life he would strive for, no matter what the cost was.

***

He had to switch schools due to the distance between his uncle's house and the school district, and he decided he would remain secluded from the other students unless entirely necessary. He didn't want to get into trouble or find his location compromised due to poor decision-making. He had some outbursts before his father was arrested and he felt even more apprehensive after, but he knew that he had to hold it together for his sister. He tried paying attention in his classes and demonstrated his best efforts to complete his work on time, despite the cacophonous environment in which he lived. He wanted nothing more than to be completely average.

But then he noticed a trio- a teacher's pet named Shauna Rivera, what appeared to be a tomboy who went by their last name, Johnson, and Johnson's boyfriend, Angus Briar. There was something special about seeing these three around the school, whether they were eating their lunch in the hallway outside the cafeteria or trying to catch each other while transitioning between classes. Angus seemed to be relatively aggressive towards Johnson as he tugged him this way and that, telling him what he could and couldn't do, or becoming jealous when he was around men who weren't him. Something about this struck a chord within him, perhaps reminding him of his sister and their father.

He was angry to see Angus and Johnson together, which eventually blurred into him becoming angry whenever he saw Angus. But he swore to himself that he wouldn't get involved. After all, these people didn't even know he existed. Why help someone if you knew for a fact that they would never help you back? But it was the blow of a punch that did it, and sure enough, he had been there to save them. It was Shauna's cries for help that caught his ear.

"Someone get help!" His head whipped around, not because of the recognition of Shauna's voice- he had never been close enough to actually hear her speak- but the pain and fear within her voice attracted his gaze towards the bodies surrounding a figure on the floor. "A teacher, a counselor- someone please!"

He told himself he wouldn't become involved. He made a promise to not just himself but also of the future in which his sister was protected. It pained him to watch a crowd congregate and so he found himself pinching his wrist as though it would snap him into a reality in which there was no violence.

"Stop it!" Shauna cried. His gaze weaved between the legs and bodies of the attackers to see Johnson, huddled with his arms around his face, and then sought out who appeared to be the leader of the army: Angus Briar.

He pinched himself harder, his fingers beginning to tremble with the force he exerted. He couldn't get involved. There was no point in getting into trouble and compromising his situation. He squeezed his eyes shut until the black static burned into his eyelids. As he opened them, he watched Shauna throw herself into the crowd and over Johnson's body. That was it.

The next thing he knew, Angus Briar was on the ground, a hand covering his eye. He felt the piercing gazes of everyone surrounding him, some of the attackers also lying on the ground. He was ground zero- the center of it all, to end it all and he knew that he had been the cause of the approaching apocalypse.

He looked over to Shauna, still cowering over Johnson's body.

"Hey," he called.

He imagined what would happen if he had done the same to his father when he caught him on top of his sister. He thought of the song of gratitude he would receive as though there was never any pain to experience in the first place, as though violence would have erased the events that would eventually lead to so much anguish. And he would say, "You're welcome." He didn't realize he had said it aloud, but he embraced it. Although it may have made him appear narcissistic, he meant it. They were welcome- welcome to his protection.

He didn't listen as the counselors attempted to lecture him. It didn't matter to him what they said. He already knew that violence was wrong, and if they were expecting him to feel remorse for his actions, they were wasting his time. His knuckles were bruised, and he thought of when his father would do the same. *Oh no,* he thought. *Am I turning into my father?* He thought of how he would listen to his grandfather yell at his father and uncle until his death. He thought of how poorly they had been treated and then how poorly they treated him. He would be able to protect others, but would he be able to protect them against him? Could he protect himself against what was brewing inside his mind? Id (noun)— the instinct of selfishness.

***

He was uncertain how long he had lain with the bodies, but he knew that he had to get moving if he wanted to get home safely. Which direction had he come from? He wished he had any sense of instinct that would guide him, but the only conclusion he came to was that if he headed in any direction, he was sure to leave the woods eventually. Was he capable of finding food, water, or shelter? He decided he would tackle that when the time came. After the past events, he found it painful to even think of putting food down his stomach. How vast were these woods exactly? It was possible that the teacher had mentioned, but he had not been paying close attention. He tried locating the sun and estimating the time of day to head into what could possibly be the direction from which he came.

He had made plenty of mistakes in his life, and many mistakes had been made on his behalf. He was certain that the entirety of his existence was a mistake in itself. But he doubted that any mistakes contained within his life had been nearly as monumental as those made within these woods. As he walked, he observed the trees around him. Mistakes in the trees would simply regrow at the wound. The leaves would shed annually, and new life would surface and expand. Should a boulder find its way nestled at the base of the trunk, it would be swallowed after enough years. He wondered whether this was something he would be able to imitate, but knew that he was far from a tree, and the pain he inflicted upon himself was unhealthy and would only cut him down further.

What life would grow from the death of his friends? What would he gain knowing they would never get to graduate high school or continue onto higher education or find love and have whatever number of children they desire? What would he gain, having robbed his friends of the opportunity to grow old and learn from their own mistakes until they find peace in their lives? What would he gain knowing they died in fear? He felt as though he no longer deserved the life he longed for, caring for his sister. He was not worthy. But he decided to endure anyway, as he was absolutely certain that it was the life his sister deserved.

Leaves snapped behind him, crackling as though their stems were bones waiting to be crushed. "You're going the wrong way, you know," a voice called. It was a deep voice, although rather weak with a crackly rasp.

Ethan turned around to see an older man standing behind him. After the events with his friends and the doppelgangers, he wasn't entirely certain he could trust this man. He felt his fingers reach for his wrist.

Still, curiosity led him. "Who are you?" he asked.

"I'm sorry for startling you. My name is Howard. Howard Lewis." Ethan expected him to hold out a hand to be shaken, but he simply stood there. "You shouldn't be in these woods, child," he told him.

It irked him that he had just been called a child, but he chose to ignore it. He hadn't asked for his name in response, and so he decided to take the initiative to provide it himself. "I'm Ethan," he said. "Do you know how to get out of these woods?"

He nodded, gesturing in a direction. "If you come across a river, you're going to want to follow it downstream," he instructed. "Whole thing is a mountain, you know, so it would be best for you to go downhill, no matter where you go."

"Thank you." Ethan thought for a few moments. He thought it was awfully strange that this man seemed to be so comfortable in the woods. "What are you doing here?" he inquired.

"You've seen them, haven't you?" Howard asked him. "I can tell by the look on your face." Ethan felt his heart press forward into his ribs with each pulse. "I know that look. I once bore a look like that. They're smart, you know. They know exactly what they need to do to get to ya."

"They killed my friends." He conveniently left out the description of shooting Johnson with the flare gun.

"Awful creatures. Absolutely horrible," Howard muttered. "Curses to the God who created them."

"What are they?"

"That's what I've been trying to figure out here," he explained. "I've been studying them for some time now."

"I thought it was just bears in the woods."

"Wouldn't that be a pleasant timeline to live in?" Howard reflected, adding a dry cough to the end of his statement like punctuation.

The cough echoed but failed to yield a response. "How do I know you're not one of them?" Ethan asked, hoping that whatever answer it produced would not be offensive or evoke danger.

"You've never seen me before, have ya?" Howard asked. Ethan shook his head. "Then you know I'm the real thing. They can only take the shape of someone you already know." He continued to hack, taking deep gulps of air between them as though he was drowning on land.

"Take the shape? What the hell do you mean?"

"You've seen them, haven't you, boy?" he sneered. "Then you must know what they're capable of. You're lucky you got out alive."

Ethan opened his mouth to ask another question, only for Howard to interrupt him.

"Listen kid, this isn't what I want you to take away from what I've said. If I were you, I would quit blabbering and leave already. These things are dangerous. You need to get out of here as quickly as you can."

"Just one last question," he pleaded. Howard took a deep breath and shook his head, enabling the question. "What do you know about them?"

"Let's hope you'll never have to find out more than you have," he responded. He began to walk away, only for Ethan to catch up to him and place a hand on his shoulder.

"Tell me," he demanded.

Howard turned and placed two dried palms on his shoulders. "You might think I'm crazy, but you've seen the crazy things that have happened here, yeah?" Ethan nodded. "You've seen them change, haven't you? Seen 'em manipulate their shape and mimic the bodies of others? It won't matter the pattern or size. But they don't turn into just anyone. They have a sixth sense- a sort of wavelength that allows them to detect the activity in your brain. They'll tease themselves into your mind and dig around like maggots searching for anything to pick at. They'll know everyone you've ever loved. They'll look you right in the eye and see that twinkle you get when you think about 'em." He pointed a finger right at Ethan. "They know how to get to you. They're smart. Bastards will imitate only those who you know can hurt you. But you don't know me, and I sure as hell don't know you."

"How do I know you're not one of them and just making this up so I believe you?"

He sighed. "I suppose you don't. But would you rather believe me or live with your question unanswered?" Ethan didn't respond. "I thought so." He removed his hands from the boy's shoulders. "Now listen. These creatures are masters of manipulation. They know how to get exactly what they want and can kill you in an instant. But they like to be… entertained. They prefer to watch you suffer. That's why I haven't been able to find one. They know I'm after them."

"What do you want with them?"

"Too many questions, boy," he rejected, initiating his cacophonous crackling cough. "You need to run and get out of here, now. You've wasted enough time already. Go downhill. Downhill," he repeated. "Don't stop until you're clear out of the woods, and maybe, you'll make it."

"But-"

"Go!" he demanded.

"Fine!" Ethan scoffed and then stormed off downhill. The incline had been so gradual that he had hardly noticed it before. It made sense to him now that he thought of it- this was a mountain after all. Perhaps it *had* been the direction in which he was heading. He was delighted, however, as downhill meant a faster pace.

But what awaited him when he left the woods? Immediately upon being reunited he would surely get in trouble for wandering away from the group. How would he even explain what had happened to his friends? Would they label him a murderer? He imagined himself being thrown in confinement, some sort of facility to contain him until he was old enough for a real prison. He loathed to think of him being situated beside his father. And what would happen to his sister? Would they even inform her of his whereabouts? He imagined her face as they would deliver the news. He pictured hundreds of different outcomes- would she be sad or disappointed or angry? He would never be able to comfort her, regardless of what she was feeling. He would only hope that she would come to visit him. Or perhaps she would refuse to associate with him. Perhaps she would change her last name, and when people asked her about her family, she would say she doesn't have any siblings. Perhaps when peers would ask her about her brother, she would incorrectly inform them that he had died.

Perhaps that would be best, he decided. He didn't know what awaited him, but he was certain that it would not be warmth or sympathy. There would be no understanding, and there would be no tears shed for him. The best life for him would be one secluded where he couldn't taunt others with his stories of monsters that forced him to kill his friends. And yes, he was certain that he had been their murderer.

"Ethan," a voice sang from a distance. It was familiar, and for a second, he wanted to turn and run towards it as quickly as possible. The thought that his friends could still be alive resonated within him, although he knew it was futile. "Ethan, what have you done?" the voice continued. He recognized the voice as Shauna's. Its timbre had the same sweetness but somehow still felt sour.

But then he thought of what Howard had told him, and he thought back to the painful picture of his friends drenched in crimson beside him. This couldn't be Shauna.

"Ethan," it insisted. "Ethan, you killed us."

"Yes, Ethan," a different voice chimed in. "If it wasn't for you, we'd still be here." It was Johnson's voice this time.

"Ethan," a voice called from the other direction, this one Shauna's again.

"No, Ethan. Over here!" another voice called, this one Johnson's.

"You killed us, Ethan," the first voice called.

"You killed us," confirmed another.

"Stop it!" he shouted at them. "I-I didn't mean to!" He began running, heading downhill, understanding that this was the best way out.

"Ethan!" a voice screamed from in front of him, the sound occluding his path. "Ethan, stop it!" it cried.

The sound of Shauna's shrieking approached him from behind. "What have you done, Ethan?" it howled.

The other voices began to imitate it. "What have you done, Ethan? What have you done?"

"Stop!" he repeated, pressing his palms to his ears. "I didn't mean to! I didn't mean to!" He kept running, but the voices only crescendoed.

"You killed us, Ethan!"

"What have you done?"

"We'd still be here!"

"You're a monster!"

The voices overlapped, each one louder than the next, as though it was a competition. Some accused, others simply screamed, a composite of beast and human as though something had tampered with the sound waves as they were produced. Regardless, they were unmistakably the voices of his friends. The sudden realization hit him that they could have tampered with the corpses, somehow. He imagined approaching Johnson and Shauna from behind, only for them to turn around, revealing bloody mouths and jagged teeth.

They would surround the bodies of the true Johnson and Shauna, now completely unrecognizable due to the merciless creatures. And he would never know the true faces of the killers. But then they became the most familiar.

His throat became tight. His shoulders bounced as they sobbed as though the power within his wails puppeted his body. The tightness in his throat expelled. "Kill me!" he felt himself cry, but realized that he had not been the one to shout. He brought his hand to his mouth to assure that it was not producing sound.

"Stop it!" he responded.

"I killed them!" another voice moaned.

"You killed me!" a Johnson accused.

The voices layered over each other to the point where they were indistinguishable- simply a cacophonous sound that would never leave his mind. He pinched his wrist and squeezed his eyes shut, trying to ground himself and understand the truth behind what was happening. He didn't kill his friends- it was all a coincidence.

"Murderer!"
He needed to leave the woods before they killed him.

"Kill me!"

He needed to-

"What have you done, Ethan?"

His own voice, but sour.

"Kill me!"

He needed to leave.

They began to scream.

He pressed his palms to his eyes, feeling the tears that had been brewing leak into the lines of his hands. He tried to keep running, but he couldn't see. He pulled his hands away but only saw through the blurs of his tears. He struck a tree and fell backwards.

"Ethan, you killed us!"

"What have you done?"

"Kill me!"

"I'd like to think…

He couldn't breathe.

"…that someday I would blossom into a rose."

His lips parted.

The Basics of Evolution

By Jork Gjeilo, PhD

Evolution is a term you may have heard of, whether referring to something in biology or simply something changing. The term refers to the development of specific characteristics over a period of time. Within biology, this can mean species acquiring different *adaptations* to help them survive in their natural habitats in the most optimal manner. This can include adapting characteristics to help catch prey or avoid predators. This is able to occur thanks to *genetic mutation,* which allows for more variation in the gene pool and therefore introduces genes that can be bred. Oftentimes this refers back to "survival of the fittest," which enables those who are most well-evolved to survive while others may perish or become unfavorable mates.

It was originally believed that evolution happened throughout the lifetime rather than over years upon years of evolution. For example, one may find some readings that refer to the giraffe's neck in this manner, often depicting them with short necks at birth, but elongating throughout their lifespan in order to reach leaves off of trees. Now, as we understand evolution more, we have come to learn that giraffes were simply deemed more fit for survival depending on the length of their neck and would therefore go on to breed further, only for the cycle to repeat itself and crank out a long-necked mammal.

There has also been plenty of research conducted on birds of paradise and how they might vary depending on the islands on which they live. This could affect many of their physical attributes, such as wing span, color, and size, but the most notable was the beak. Due to differentiation between prey on the various islands, birds evolved beaks that best suited the environment. This could include developing a thin pointed beak for insects, or perhaps a larger curved beak for fruits and buds. Regardless, it is interesting to see the different adaptations demonstrating themselves in closely related species.

Evolution is a constant balancing act as it develops prey that can escape predators and then predators that may feast on the prey. The world becomes more varied, more dangerous, but also more exciting when evolution is about. We have come to understand how humans have evolved over time much better, which is able to pose the question of what will happen to humans in the future. What will change about us, and what in nature will create these changes?

Chapter Thirteen

I'm attempting to see the good in a world without you and finding it much more difficult than anticipated, but I know you would want me to try, and so I shall.

She couldn't believe that Doug would have tried to convince her to leave with him. How shallow did he think she was? Wife or no wife, he was a suspicious person, and so adulterated on top of that. She found herself wandering through the woods trying to decipher why someone like him would be in the woods in the first place, but her mind came up blank. She needed something to clear her mind of him. Would she think of Jessica Heathers? She decided to leave those events in the past. What about her mother? There was no bringing her back. But what about her father? What about poor Jim Brown, who only cared for his daughter unconditionally when his wife left him?

She thought about how hard he had worked his entire life just to be able to support the family. She had always favored her mother, perhaps out of instinct, but she knew how much her father had cared for her, whether it be working night shifts or working from home, or working with his heart condition. He was always there. She thought about when she was in high school and thinking of pursuing higher education, but understood how her father would have to possibly pick up another job in order to provide for her. She had been working too, but only part-time due to her schedule. She would later move to full-time and stay in retail for another six years before moving to a secretarial job.

She never moved out of the house for fear of the day that Jim would not be able to care for himself. The day had not yet come, but she heard it humming in the distance. He would have to exercise more in order to maintain his health, and there had been quite a few occasions in which he overexerted himself or twisted something painfully, leaving Clara to monitor him more closely. He had to change his diet, and while he used to cook more often, Clara was taking it up, abiding by the new rules and numbers that would keep her father safe. She would sometimes check up on him while he was having a particularly rough day at work, understanding that stress would worsen his condition. She felt as though she would remain beside her father until the end of his life.

But what would happen after that? She could stay in the same town in the same house working the same job, but was that what she wanted? She could travel the world, just as she always had hoped. She could hike every corner, just as she had planned to do before Jessica Heathers left her. She could try to work to put herself through college. The possibilities were endless, and there wouldn't be anyone from her past holding her back from who she felt she was meant to be. She felt selfish thinking about her father's possible heart failure, but knew that she would have to prepare for it in some way. She knew it was healthy for her to visit these woods, too. It would be beneficial for her to escape her father for some time while also giving him room to breathe on his own. He would only have to work for himself, even if for just a little bit.

Dampening footsteps interrupted her thoughts.

"Doug, I swear to God-" she began before she realized that the figure approaching her was another man. He was older and looked as bad as he smelled. He seemed reluctant to approach her but found himself near her.

"Not another one," he murmured under his breath.

"Excuse me?" she responded, only catching shards of the words he spoke.

"You need to leave," he told her, projecting his gravelly voice more this time. "It's not safe here."

"I'm aware of the hostile conditions of these woods," she told him confidently. "I've read about them and I'm prepared to deal with them."

"You don't understand!" he began, not finishing before Clara jutted in.

"I don't understand? I've been reading about this place for years! I've been observing it, longing for this expedition for over ten years! I know what I've gotten myself into and I plan on finishing it!" she argued.

"There are creatures!" He was raising his voice now, quickly growing tired of the ignorance of his conversers. "They'll kill you!"

Clara thought back to what Doug had said about his wife dying. He also believed it to be at the hand of some gruesome creature. But such things were the content of myths and folktales. Sure, there were such tales surrounding these woods, but believing them would be to believe that the boogeyman still lurked under your bed. Still, curiosity and a pinch of humor lured her in.

"What creatures?" she asked. Her curiosity led her, pulling her by the throat. She knew about all of the folklore surrounding the mountains but attributed it all to superstition. She didn't even realize that her body had aimed itself back in the man's direction. "What do you know about that?"

"Does it matter?" the man bit back. "They're here and they're going to try to kill ya!"

"Well, if you don't tell me about them, why would I want to leave because of them?"

The man took a deep breath. "I'm sorry," he apologized. "I've been trying to get people out of these woods for far longer than I should have. But you are right- I do owe you an explanation even though you've got a thick skull. So I'll tell you so that I can get you out of this damned place!"

He began to speak, his vocabulary changing entirely as though it had all been rehearsed. It was clear he believed this to be his truth. "This world has slowly been spiraling into despair. Human activity has caused an increase in pollution and other unnatural emissions. It's come to the point where environments are becoming unideal or unlivable for us as well as other creatures around us. Normally, we'd be able to adapt to such things, but we're changing things so quickly that we are unable to evolve in time to overcome the mess we've created. One of these effects you can witness all around you- the freezing nights and scorching days- all of this weather has to do with human activity."

"I know this already," Clara interjected. "And the mountains were created from the collision of tectonic plates and the trees still receive enough nutrients from the surroundings. These woods are entirely unique in nature. It's bad but it's not the end of the world."

"Let me speak," the man demanded. She felt it best not to respond. "Years and years ago I worked for a corporation tasked with finding the **Cure**. There are so many burdens on humanity and they- *we* all thought we would be able to find an answer. We endeavored, researching all corners of the planet as we knew to be able to find it. Every branch of science had come together for this one cause- this one **cure**- and we were all definite that we would find it. It can be so hard to find new information. So often we're given the facts and are limited by them. We simply see them as reality rather than what does not yet exist.

"And so we started over. We started overturning every aspect of life as we knew it so we would be able to view things from a different angle. We started asking 'why' and 'how' to everything we could possibly imagine. We even enlisted the help of some toddlers- they're absolute experts in questioning life around them. Their eyes and brains are still fresh. They're still constantly searching for new information to learn. None of this helped. We thought we had hit a brick wall. We thought it was impossible for there to be a **cure** after years and years of research. We tried joining together in as many combinations as we possibly could and then we tried some on our own. Anything that would alter our state of mind in any sort of way.

"And finally, I found it. I found the **Cure**. At least I thought I had. It was the sweet spot- all of the equations and properties blended together perfectly into what I presumed to be the **Cure**. B-but my love-" He began to choke on his words. "She- she wanted a more h-humane way to test it out. She loved every aspect of this planet and so she wanted to p-protect it in any way she could. She didn't want me to test on the animals, but I knew that-that in order for us to advance it would have to happen. There had to be a way around this where we would both be happy.

"So my love volunteered. She went against all of the rules. I- I should have told her no, but she was so convincing. I loved her so much and every word she spoke was intoxicating. I thought I could trust her, but even worse, I thought I could trust myself. I thought I could trust my math and my research and the facts I had accrued. And so I allowed her to volunteer to receive the **Cure**- the **Cure** to the world around us- how we would be able to maneuver the hostile world we had been born into which only withered away at our own hands.

"I watched her slowly drift away. It was her mind first, and her body next. One day she was speaking to me of the expanses of the universe and took me with her through the billions of layers of the galaxies so vividly as though we were some sort of astral projectors journeying to the furthest corner of the universe. The next day, she struggled to remember her name, her eyes narrowing- the syllables resting on the tip of her tongue, taunting her as they shooed away mercilessly. Within a month, she was forced to leave work for the hospital, barely able to remember her own name at this point. This was when she began having physical struggles.

"The day she was admitted, she wobbled into the facility, one of the nurses ushering another over to provide a wheelchair for her. She would never stand again after that. I never thought I would look upon the short walk from the lot to the front desk so fondly as though it was the closest to progress she would taste in a while. I would try to visit her as often as I could, but unfortunately, I had to pay the bills somehow. And so I only saw her on the weekends. It seemed as though every weekend she had a different tube in her- catheters, feeding tubes, ventilators. She couldn't speak, but her eyes- her eyes told me everything. She didn't want to be on this planet anymore. She didn't want to be hooked up to so many machines, relying on their hard work for her existence. I cannot pinpoint the day she was gone- the day she left her conscience entirely, sending it like a balloon into the mesosphere, towards the moon, and allowing her to expand across the universe, just as she always had wanted. I pulled the plug on her.

"For a while, this caused me to fall out in my work. I didn't want anything to do with this '**cure**' that had robbed me of my beautiful wife. My hands were the hands of a murderer, and I thought to myself how much purer the world would be if I chopped them off. But I knew that she would have wanted me to endure and endeavor, and so I returned to my research eventually. I, however, did not grant her wishes and chose to test my next **cure** on animals. I knew she would have disapproved greatly, but I could not risk any other choice. I wasn't even supposed to test on any human in the first place.

"I thought back to earlier research I had done on various animals and their abilities to adapt to their environment and considered what would happen if humans were able to replicate this themselves. But with the world around us diminishing so drastically, I knew that the power of these creatures would not be enough. We had to isolate the senses and understand the world around us in so much depth that we could overcome anything that would come our way if we wanted a true **cure**-a **cure** from the environment-a **cure** from plague-a **cure** from *mortality*."

He interjected his story with a hack, his cough rattled in his throat, and for a brief moment. He paused, and a few puffs of breath pumped through his chest again until a rumble of coughs emerged once again. Clara suspected he might faint. But he continued.

"I began testing on small animals, and after a few trials, the results were promising. Unfortunately, this is when I began having visions. It seemed as though the closer I got to finding the **Cure**, the closer I felt to my beloved. In hindsight, I can understand how ridiculous this may have seemed and how bizarre I must have appeared. But in the moment of the occurrences, I can assure you that she was just as tangible as I am to you. This clouded my sense of reality greatly, and I unfortunately became reckless.

"And with that came some miscalculations. I made these creatures far too strong, almost as though it was brilliance being consumed by the darkest mold. My **cure** cured too much! But by this point, I had begun my research testing on wolves. And these wolves began changing their forms, not just their skin. They were not just adapting to the temperature of the environment as originally planned, but were able to mimic their prey or their loved ones, or their enemies. This wasn't immediately apparent to me as they were confined and therefore lived their entire lives only knowing other wolves and myself. When one of them had presented itself in the form of me, I had assumed it to be a vision and cursed my brain for brewing such a sight.

"And their senses- they were able to sense the environment so well that they could see into the other's cognitions. They were seeing on the same exact wavelengths to the extent where their neurons were able to communicate with each other. And so they were able to see my thoughts and understand them and take on the shape of those whom I fear- those whom I love. So, when I looked in the cage and saw my beloved among these mind-boggling wolves, I threw myself into the cage to rescue her. But alas, this was the mind of the wolves working towards their escape. They had fooled me- made a pawn of me. And so that night, they all escaped into these very woods, able to change their form and use your mind as inspiration for whatever that form may be.

"I came here, hoping I would be able to kill them myself. Although I must admit that after everything I've been through, and understanding exactly how powerful and manipulative these creatures are, I wish they would end me, themselves. I am but one man. I cannot kill them all. And so, I wish they would end my suffering once and for all. But of course, they are able to see into my mind, and so they know that is what I wish for the most. They've been keeping me alive to taunt me- allow me to dwell in this horrible situation I have created and lost my wife to. I fear they will use my loss of will to live against me."

Clara had no idea what to think. This man was clearly insane. He admitted to having visions, which was a red flag in itself. He spoke in such a passionate manner that she imagined it would have convinced somebody. But she knew that whoever that somebody was, it would not be her.

"I'm so sorry," she told him. "I'm sorry for your loss of wife and uh... will to live." She thought of how to phrase this. "But I simply have a hard time grasping all of this... information," she admitted.

"As you would," he responded, beginning to hack away. This was clearly the most he had spoken in quite some time. "But I have faith now. I have faith that you will come to your senses before they sense you. I have faith that you will make it out of these woods safe and sound." He reached out for her hand, but she instinctively pulled back. "I cannot convince you to trust me or my word, but I can assure you that this is the truth. And with that, I shall leave you. Nothing more that I say can convince you."

Clara decided not to respond, but to simply nod. A nod would indicate confirmation, but remain vague as to what it was confirming. She did not want to insult his story, and knew it would be rude of her to disclose this to him. And so she left it at that nod.

"Good luck," he told her. "I hope that you can keep my story with you and use it to guide you."

"Thank you," she responded. "Goodbye."

And with that, she turned and left, leaving him alone once again. He had grown used to loneliness. Not only that, but he felt as though he deserved it. It was a punishment to him for everything he had done his entire life. But he realized after Clara was long gone that he was not truly alone. He heard light footsteps and did not have to turn to know who it was.

"My love," he greeted. "It has been quite some time, has it not?"

Chapter Fourteen

And so, I'm trying my best, as difficult as it may be, to forgive myself and leave it all in the past.

"Well, maybe we're just… very different people!"

"Well, maybe we are." She started towards the door. It happened so quickly, but so slow at the same time. He watched every joint moving as she walked as though she was trudging through molasses. She was full of grace, despite her raging anger. He loved her so much, and as she traveled across the room, he began to see flashes of everything he had fallen in love with her for her auburn hair, the fire in her spirit, the way her voice sounded like honey. He couldn't lose her.

"Where are you going?" he asked, terrified. He saw their futures together fading away and wanted to grasp at the fragments of light that created them. "Stop! Where are you going?"

And the door closed. He was uncertain whether it would open again, and so he sat on the couch waiting, hoping that she would return. He replayed the scenes over in his mind, hoping that he could redo them and mend the mistakes he had made. But he knew that no matter how hard he wished, he did not possess the ability to turn back time. This did not prevent him from ruminating, though, as he grew intoxicated with the last few traces of her voice poisoning his mind.

There was a knock at the door, and before the second knock came, he realized he had already been so quick to stand up. He ran to the door, thinking about how he would be so grateful to hold his love in his arms once again. He thought of everything he would do differently to ensure their happiness going forward. But when he swung the door open, there was a different iteration of his love in front of him- one who wore heavy amounts of makeup and dressed as though she were the recipient of an award.

"Oh," he said, not even thinking about what effect this might have on his visitor.

"Oh?" she mimicked. "Is that how you greet all of your guests?"

He sighed and pressed his lips together as though it would hold back all of the unkind things he wished to say to her.

"Are you going to invite me in?" she prompted. He held the door open and allowed her to step into the room.

"She's not here," he told her, uncertain how many details he should provide. He decided the fewer the better, yet found himself elaborating by saying, "Not sure when she'll be back, though."

"I just came to return something," she informed, holding up something he didn't care to look at. "I'll take some tea, by the way," she demanded.

She continued into their home, removing her coat and pressing it into his arms all in one swift, natural motion. She placed herself neatly on the couch and crossed her legs. He supposed he didn't have a choice as to whether she was going to stay, and definitely no control over how long. He would simply have to endure whatever she would throw his way.

***

"I take it you have no siblings?" she asked him. He shook his head but knew that his response would not alter

195

her continuation. "You must not understand what it's like-mine and Macie's relationship. I can't imagine what you think of me." He smiled to himself, knowing exactly what he felt about her. "The truth is," she cupped her tea in her palms as though she was attempting to ward off the chilling wind of a truth. "I've always looked up to Macie. I've always been inspired by what she's done and wanted to take after her in some ways. I always try to do what I can to make her proud, you know?"

He looked at her as though he was seeing her as an actual person for the first time- and perhaps he was.

"I'm sorry about what I said to you the first night we met. Telling you about her past love life. That's something she should disclose to you at her own will. I shouldn't have said anything." She stirred the remains of the tea and honey in her cup, the spoon clinking as it collided with the confines of the porcelain. "I suppose I'm just a tad bit... jealous," she admitted, articulating the consonants. "Macie found love like yours on the first try. It's not something that happens to everyone."

He took a deep breath, understanding that it would be best for him to respond now. He had been mostly quiet all night, and if his words counted at all, this would be the time in which they were worth the most. "You'll find someone," he started, realizing how entirely cliche it sounded as the words left his lips. "When I saw Macie for the first time, I just knew there was something special about her. I've had feelings about other people I've met- you just look at them and know they're special. But with her, I saw her and saw all of our future flash before our eyes. It was like a secret was unlocked, and the world was ready for me to know my destiny. It's a feeling I don't think comes around often, but it's one I'm sure you'll find."

He continued on. "I don't feel like I deserve her. We have our differences- everyone does. I know that there are so many things that she'll accomplish that I'll never even imagine seeing in myself. She has so much fire, and I want her to be with me wherever she chooses to spread it. Someday, you'll find someone like this, too. You'll look at them and just know that you are destined to be together, whether you deserve it or not."

She threw herself at him, pressing her moist, lipstick-smeared lips against his. He pushed her away by the cheek before she could even position herself comfortably. "Nope," he responded, making it very obvious that he was not interested. He even wiped his lips with the back of his hand, feeling the slime of her kiss spread across his skin. "You should go now."

***

Nightfall was approaching like the rumble of thunder, and he knew that he was far from the edge of the woods, despite him having no sense of where he was. He had anticipated he was headed in the right direction, but the amount of time he was walking argued against him, and he knew he would have to set up camp if he wanted to stay safe. He couldn't tell if he was traveling faster or slower without Macie, but knew that he still had time to determine what his alibi would be. He considered simply telling the truth, but recalled how well that had gone over with his last interaction with Clara and decided otherwise. Clara had mentioned the hostility of the woods. Perhaps he could simply blame it on that.

He curled up in his tent, snow beginning to sprinkle from the trees as though the hefty leaves had birthed them. There was something ominous about their descent that he couldn't quite place, hence why he had decided to remain indoors. He was exhausted, hungry, and thirsty. He and Macie had packed more food, but she had been the one to carry it. He was too preoccupied with disposing of her body and planning that he hadn't even thought of food. He had simply thought of how quickly he needed to escape, rather than how long he would remain in the woods.

And so, he turned onto his back, demonstrating his best attempt to ignore the groaning from his stomach, the dryness of his mouth, or the ache behind his eyes. Things would be different when he got back home, for sure. He would move into a small apartment- perhaps even consider a retirement community. He was getting rather old and felt his joints slowing with the occasional creak or pop if he moved them unfavorably. Retirement sounded pleasant; he was sick of low-paying odd jobs anyway. There had been so many jobs he had taken on to be able to provide for him and Macie, and they had been saving up for their retirement. If there were such a thing as a sign from the universe, this would be it, disregarding how gruesome it was.

But suddenly the unmistakable sound of footsteps crinkling the foliage beneath it brought him immediately to his feet. He knew who it had to be. They had run into each other twice already. Surely, she had come to her senses and would assist him out of these woods. His heart rate increased as he pictured the two of them escaping once and for all. He pulled the drape of his tent open and saw her standing there.

"Clara!" he greeted.

"Hi, Doug," she responded, her hands on the straps of her backpack. He watched as crystals of snow clung to the soft curly tresses of her hair. There was a whisper of silence. A snowflake nestled itself in her eyelash. "Can I come in?" she asked him. He nodded, leaving space for her in the tent intended for two people, albeit a different companion.

She unzipped her parka and placed her backpack in the corner. It wasn't much warmer in the tent, but she seemed inclined to remove her layers around company.

"So do you believe me?" he began after they had sat in silence for a sufficient amount of time. He wondered whether he should elaborate further. "About my wife?" He wasn't sure whether he would regret mentioning her again after witnessing the reaction she had, but knew that the truth was more important in this scenario.

She nodded. He was able to get a better look at her now without her parka. Besides her long eyelashes that shaded her light brown eyes, she had beautiful, smooth skin- a color he could not pinpoint. She seemed relatively fit and some of her curls were confined to neat braids. Her lips were luscious as though she were the doll of a young girl's dreams. He had known she was beautiful before, but now she appeared much more radiant.

"I barely survived them," she explained to him. "They almost got me, and I just barely managed to escape."

"Did you see them?"

"No, but I could hear them."

"What were they saying?" She shot him a look that indicated she was still panicked, and he realized elaboration was not the path to follow here. "Sorry," he told her.

"Doug?" she started. He looked up at her, his gaze locking in her beautiful brown eyes. "What are you doing out here?"

He knew that now was the time for the truth. No matter what it might bring, he knew it was the safest route for him. "I came out here to mend my relationship with my wife." He pondered on elaboration once more. He decided to tuck this one in his back pocket.

"But you're all alone now?"

He nodded.

"Does it bother you?" she asked him. "Do you want to be alone?"

"I don't think anyone ever *wants* to be alone. Some people might convince themselves that they do, but I don't think anyone ever *wants* it."

"Doug," she started, her voice becoming hoarse, her eyes drifting off into her peripherals. She refocused and placed a hand on his cheek. "Do you still want me?" she asked him. He was surprised, and it took him a few moments to comprehend what she was asking of him, but he eventually lost himself in her eyes and nodded.

She pulled herself closer to him, the heat of another body serving as a comfort and addiction. Her kiss felt familiar- he wondered if it was because she was meant to be someone important to him, if they were linked together in any sort of way where their kiss simply made sense in the scheme of the universe. He had heard the term "sparks flying" before and knew that this instance was exactly what it had intended to depict.

He placed a hand on her back to draw her closer, his other hand on her cheek, his fingers intruding into her hairline. It was just as soft as he had imagined. She retreated for a second, pressing her forehead to his. She planted a kiss on his nose and migrated downwards. She reached his trousers and looked up at him, smiling. But something was amiss.

Her teeth were barbed and rugged as though someone had bashed rocks together until they fit into place. There were several rows of them, each with at least thirty or forty of the jagged whites stuffed into the gums. As she pulled further away, an odor began to emerge from her breath that had not existed earlier. She stank of mud, sour fruit, and rotten hard-boiled eggs. He imagined foods being shredded by the jetties of her teeth, shards becoming lodged in between the uneven surfaces.

Her eyes were jet black as though ink had flooded them. He imagined them swelling up like a boil, and saw the black liquid spilling out in tears with the prick of a pin. He wondered how she could possibly see with such an occlusion- if she could even see at all. He could see himself in the glossy reflection as though his image was the closest thing to humanity the eyes would ever perceive. What expression did she wear? He suspected it might be something sinister, considering the teeth and pigmentation. He felt as though the eyes stared right through him, poking a hole into his stomach and allowing all of the slimy details of his entrails surface, exposing parts of him to the world he would never have anticipated would see the light of day.

And then he began to smell something even more rancid. He fixated on her skin- originally smooth, absolutely flawless, and beautiful- now sizzling and bubbling. He watched as the different layers exposed themselves, each one peeling and scorching away as though it was a page of a book in the center of a flame it never intended to see. Her skin made her appear as though she was pulling her flesh inside-out, the muscles beneath her skin now peeking through. She took her fingers, which were now frothing like beaten egg whites, and she grabbed herself by the lips and tore, the skin peeling as though it had been made out of clay. He gawked in terror at the splotches of skin that had once been pristine and the rows of crooked, sharp teeth that had been concealed behind pink, opulent lips. Where had Clara gone? He tried to piece together what was left, but could only see the outlines of what used to be.

The true devastation set in with a drop in Doug's stomach as the structure of her face, hidden beneath the naked muscles and teeth, everything scrambling away as though she had maggots under her face. Everything about her face was alive, her teeth now becoming offset to the point where they intercepted each jutting out like a bundle of stakes gathered in a frantic fistful. Still her eyes remained until her hands, now dissolving like melted provolone and dripping off of her figure, pulled away at her eyelids, the remaining skin and muscle ripping away with a horrible gush, and her eyes rolling back into her head as though they had never been attached but were rather eight-balls awaiting the cue to knock them into place.

Her hands, dripping acidic flesh, placed themselves on either side of what he could barely refer to as her head and abruptly jerked her skull with a ripple of snaps to an awkward angle, causing her to resemble a broken marionette. Her fingers began to lurch as though they were being operated by millions of creatures until they constructed themselves into sharp claws. The center of her back snapped, sending the top of her torso in a different direction from her lower back, curving her into a slither until her spine crackled and wrinkled into an arc. Her arms lurched as though her shoulders were sending them in the wrong direction, and she toppled to the ground, causing him to wonder whether he should approach her.

Every time he thought one horror would end, another would begin. Her neck began to elongate as though she were attempting to catch a better look at him from afar. Her knees reversed into an awkward shape, the backs of her legs following the crooked contour of her back. And bones continued to restructure, each one producing a painful crack and snap. Finally, they all finished revealing a congregation of every haunting horror before him. He was entirely frozen with fear. Was this still Clara? Was this the very thing that had attacked Macie?

He wanted to run, but his legs wouldn't carry him anywhere. He felt his knees quivering and thought they might buckle underneath him, making him easy prey for whatever creature was before him. He realized he had been holding his breath this entire time and began to feel lightheaded. It was as though he had gasped in terror at the first sight and had only continued to inhale as the frights continued to erupt.

He picked up his left leg, wobbling as though his body was already limp, and took a step towards the opening of the tent. The creature lunged, and he found himself carrying his body as recklessly as he could, trying his hardest not to look back at whatever was following him. He didn't make it far before it sank its talons deep into his back, anchoring his body down to the ground like a chain. He tried to reach for a tree root in front of him, but found difficulty wielding his arms. He would not be able to save himself.

He felt the breath of the creature on his neck and even detected a bit of the putrid odor that flowed from its mouth. The last thing he saw was a woman's hand reaching out for him through a bright light. He imagined the rest of his life with this woman; he saw the entirety of their relationship in a flash, understanding that whoever was taking him was going to take care of him and ensure he would never feel agony such as this again. Would he see her once more? He heard a sour whisper.

"I thought you loved me."

Chapter Fifteen

Perhaps when we meet again someday, I can tell you about all of the wonderful things I have found in the world, with and without you.

There are certain fragments of life that only make sense after time and reflection have been applied, such as allowing rivers to flow into the ocean. Sometimes it takes the constant reconnection of thoughts to form clarity in a concoction of constant repetition. Other times it simply takes aging like a fine wine or cheese until the thought has ruminated long enough to make sense finally. Then comes the inquiry of how one could have possibly missed the details - how they hadn't come to an earlier comprehension. Some may kick themselves over their lack of awareness, but in truth, everyone has their own pace that must be respected in the scheme of realization.

While Clara continued on her journey, still somewhat annoyed at Doug's intrusion, she thought back to one particular moment that always tickled her when reflecting on the abandonment by her mother. Jim had begun sleeping on the couch- it was something that confused Clara at first until she came to realize he had chosen to leave the bedroom untouched. Others would have immediately disposed of all of the wife's belongings, given the situation, but he had chosen to leave the room absolutely pristine in hopes that it would await her should she ever decide to return.

Clara had missed her mother greatly. She finally understood the joy that stemmed from her visitations between journeys. The loneliness that arose from her absence only strengthened her longings, drawing her attention away from any of the excess stress Jim endured. And so, on days in which she chose not to sit beside her father as he quietly worked away at whatever he was doing that week, she decided to explore the confines of her parents' abandoned room, hoping to find something that would connect her to her mother in some way or another.

She had never spent much time in her parents' room, understanding the line of privacy within the frame of the door, but she had memories burned into her mind of what it had looked like in the few instances in which she had entered. She recalled them as she snuck over to the door, hoping her father would not hear her entry. He knew that should he go looking for her, this would be the last place he would expect. And so, she continued on, closing the door behind her before inspecting the room.

She inspected the bed first. The sheets were lopsided, pulled to the cover on one side and hanging off the bed on the other. She couldn't imagine who slept on either side, but imagined her father would have wanted to keep the bed just as his wife had left it, and so she labelled the unmade side as her mother's. She examined the nightstands on either side, each one holding a lamp and some keepsakes; the one on her side presented a framed photograph of the family from when Clara was quite young. She could not recall the events of the photograph and assumed she had been too young to remember.

She picked it up and took note of the exact location and angle it had been placed, but the bare wood exposed where a sheet of dust was bare, outlining it for her. She looked at her mother's face and how young and happy she had been in the photo. Her hair was just as curly as she had remembered and her smile was incredibly infectious. She took note of the color in her father's hair and only now realized how dull it had become. Had it been from old age or stress or his heart condition? She could not determine. She replaced the frame and continued onwards.

She began opening the dresser drawers, taking note of which ones were empty and which ones were not as familiar to her. Her father had moved most of his clothes to a closet in the office so he could avoid revisiting the bedroom, so she knew that those had to belong to him. The unfamiliar clothes she expected were her mother's. She had seen her father bearing a multitude of outfits, seemingly the only changing aspect of him. But her mother had not been home often enough for Clara to memorize her wardrobe.

She removed a yellow blouse from the top of one of the dressers, examining every detail she possibly could- the slight scratch of the fabric, the billowy silhouette, the small white buttons, and the thin collar. She had never seen her mother wear it but she pictured it vividly in her head and knew that she would have been beautiful. And then there it was- the scent of oranges that had become so addicting to her, even after her disappearance months ago. She brought it closer to her, inhaling slowly and deep, allowing the sweet scent to infiltrate her body as though it would help her become closer to her mother. It felt as though the seeds of the original orange tree had been planted within her brain, and inhaling would provide it with the oxygen it needed to grow. She folded it neatly and placed it back into the drawer.

And then she moved on to the bathroom, not expecting to find much. The shower had some products within it that she assumed had belonged to her mother. The rugs on the floor were so bleached by the sun-or perhaps from so much use-that she could not decipher what the original coloring had been. And then she decided to open the cabinets.

She had been expecting to see some products, much like in the shower, or some extra toilet paper or cleaning supplies. But what greeted her instead were decades of orange bottles, each one labelled clearly. They were not organized in any sort of way but appeared as though they had been tossed in, perhaps the user shutting the cabinet door as quickly as possible in the event the pile was disrupted too aggressively, causing it to topple over and spill onto the floor. She plucked one from the top of the pile, hoping she would not cause any avalanche, and examined the label. It had been for something called *Exartomal*, intended to be taken orally once a day. The bottle was completely empty.

She had recognized the bottle from the pharmacy and wondered what her mother had been taking and whether it had anything to do with the horrible illness that had consumed her that one week during which she had cared for her mother. That would have perhaps accounted for one bottle, but what about the others? She twisted the top open only to be completely overwhelmed with the scent of oranges.

And then Clara realized, not within her memory but within the present moment, what had happened. She was flooded with memories of her mother when she had been home, tipping pills into her mouth quite often. She would swallow them dry and as though she had been sneaking them. But she was well aware that with this many bottles, her father would have been quite conscious of the situation. The disappearances fell into place, and then the arguments, and the constant search for money. Her mother had not been a pleasant woman, she realized. She had been an addict blinded by her high, causing her to appear wonderful. Semblance (noun)– what is seen before comprehended.

Clara jumped to her feet, realizing how hard her father had worked to be able to provide for the family. She thought about the night her mother had left and how absolutely devastated he had been. She thought about the endless fights upon fights and how her father simply wanted what was best for his daughter. And then she thought about how he had tried so hard to conceal the truth from her as if it was going to protect her. She knew that she had to see him and have a real talk with him. And she finally wondered how she had not realized it after all of these years. It was time to return home to him.

She packed up her belongings and pondered whether the timing was proper or not. It had begun to rain; the fragments of sky she could see through the gathering of leaves above her demonstrated dark clouds. She felt a wind tangle itself through gaps in her clothing and entwine itself into her hair. She would have to hurry if she was going to attempt to stay dry, but she knew that the impending rain was inevitable, and she would have to cover herself. And so, she finished up, pulled some covers over her head, and started heading downhill.

Her father had gone through so much for her and she thought back to when he had attempted to convince her not to leave for this trip. She felt as though she was selfish, ignoring all of his concerns simply so she could explore somewhere and avenge the friendship that she had ruined herself. No, now was the time to admit to her mistakes and find peace in the future. Should she reach out to Jessica Heathers and apologize for what she had done, or leave the years in the past and simply be labeled as having had better days?

She noticed something in the distance- something man-made that was rather difficult to identify from far away. Part of her felt as though she should leave it as it was, but curiosity possessed her, and she found herself gravitating towards it. Something about it whispered to her like a cry for help, only discovery could quench. And so, she continued onwards until she found herself at a tent.

The trees surrounding her felt still. While they would normally sway with the breath of the wind, they were stagnant. But still she felt as though eyes were pricking her skin. She stopped to listen for any movement, but determined that whoever had set up their camp in this location had stepped away for a few moments, perhaps to find some water. The rain was beginning to trickle down, heavier drops plopping down from where the water gathered on the tips of leaves. Thirst would not be an issue at the moment and so she wondered whether she should await the return of the camper. But then she walked around to the front of the tent and was struck with horror.

There was blood on the ground, mixed in some horrible clumps of something she could not identify. She noticed footprints, and her curiosity won her over once again. She followed them, the blood pooling in dampened puddles diluted with the patterings of the rain and splattering the mess further. The humidity of the rain grasped onto the scent of the blood and pressed it against her lips so it could climb into her sinuses. As her nose came to understand the scent within it, it crawled its way down her spine, the talons digging into each vertebrae. Her heart was consumed by the smell next and it pounded as if to shoo away the scent as it gripped further into her body. Her eyes must be tricking her. There it was: a body half-consumed and fully deceased, appearing more familiar than she would have preferred. She wondered if it was possible to prefer a corpse one way or another, but the fact that she recognized the clothes on his back sent the shivers deep into her stomach like a dagger. The longer she looked, the more it would twist around in her innards. The body was face down, and she contemplated whether she should confirm her suspicions of its owner.

She found herself rolling the body, not questioning why she had determined this to be the right decision. The body rocked when she finally flipped it onto its back, the shoulder rolling with it as though it were still alive. Her fears were confirmed. There was Doug, one glossy, bloodshot eye wide open and staring into the heavens, the rest of his face consumed as though someone had pulled his skin like a slab of clay. There was so much blood that she could hardly see past the crimson that stickied her hands. His face had been the only skin succumbed to the brisk air and here it all was, fragmented like a jigsaw puzzle. He was unnaturally cold- a cold she had never felt on human flesh that sent another sensation down her body. She found herself retching but tried to hold it back. She pressed her hand to her mouth in an uneven heave, only for the blood on her hands to stain her skin. She felt filthy, as though the confirmation of his death made the situation more grotesque than the comfort of a question mark.

She examined his back, pulling up the layers of his clothing to reveal large slashes and gashes engraved into his back. They were so deep that she could start to see his bones peeking through his skin. They were shattered like broken glass, and she could even swear that she saw tooth markings on them. She looked around her to realize that fragments of his ribs had been sprinkled like a garnish, causing her to wonder what atrocities had to be committed for the strength of a human bone to be decimated so gruesomely. It reminded her of a stick of chalk.

She replaced his clothing and realized that what he had been attempting to tell her had been the truth. And then she remembered what the old man had told her about the wolves and his research. She could hear his gravelly voice echoing in her skull. She knew that, as crazy as it seemed, what he had explained had only been true as well. She was in danger, and the longer she stayed here, the more likely it was that she would wind up in a similar condition to Doug.

She began to run, just a bit clumsily, as she tried to weave her way through and around all of the nature in her path. It seemed as though the brambles' outstretched fingers of branches were attempting to pull her back into the woods. The roots became hands that grabbed at her feet, trying to trip her and yank her into the ground. She felt the burden of eyes upon her skin, and each tree felt as though it was a hovering body forcing her to feel minuscule in comparison. And the tree branches tried to blind her, along with the clouds that lurked beyond them. Rain was beginning to swoop in from the side in thick sheets, each gust of wind forcing it into her side, clashing with her and trying to stop her from escaping.

And then she finally tripped, her hands hardly catching her as she toppled to the ground. She pulled herself up, trying to ignore the soreness that arose, only to see something by her feet. She found herself in a sea of denial, the rain now yelling in her ear as it collided with her body. Lying on the floor of the woods was another corpse, this one not as familiar, but still enough to frighten her. The old man lay face-up, as though he was attempting to stargaze through the fragments of sky that shone through the treetops. His crows feet served as a reservoir for his blood, his face tainted with the color just as fresh as Doug's.

His torso looked almost like it had erupted all of the organs within it, evacuated like mucus from a wet cough. She saw shreds of his entrails scattered in the pooled blood with bites taken out of it. Whatever had been there before was now conglomerated into a new form of chunks and pieces, with the exception of his intestines, which strung out with an occasional bite left behind like a poisoned kiss. She realized that had the creatures been hungry, they would have had no hesitation in shredding their victims apart and prying each muscle apart with their fangs. This display was not out of hunger.

"I'm so sorry," she found herself whispering It continued to spill out like bile. "I'm so so so so sorry. I didn't believe you. I'm sorry! I'm so sorry!" She felt a chill creep down her arm and knew that the rain would soon become snow. Each flake would attack her as she attempted to escape this nightmare, and she would have to continue to move quickly if she wanted to emerge alive.

She continued, the relentless wind trying to pull her down. She attempted to run but found herself burdened by its hands like she was trying to shoot through rubber. She felt it trying to pull her back into the woods, leaving her uncertain whether this burden was from the weather or the guilt surfacing in her mind. It wrapped a million arms around her shoulders, keeping her hostage in a bitter embrace. She could swear she heard it whispering secrets into her ears with a cold breath. She tried to push them away but she only found herself attempting to formulate what horrible creature had reached Doug and the old man. What had that man created that was so sinister and unforgiving? Had this man pulled a creature from the depths of hell for the sake of taunting humanity's demise? What had he released into the world? She pleaded that she would not be given the chance to discover it.

And then she saw an odd figure in the distance. She knew that it was her duty to protect whomever she came across now, just as Doug and the old man had attempted to do with her. She had to redirect this person and pull them out of the woods with her before it was too late. She found herself accelerating, understanding she couldn't waste a single moment.

But then she was close enough to realize what was before her. She saw the body of a young man, perhaps seventeen or eighteen, hanging from a branch, the tightness of a rope straining his throat. His jade green eyes pierced into her own, not necessarily afraid but seeing into dimensions she could never comprehend herself. Despite the state of his body, his face appeared to be in complete peace, any creases from emotion completely smoothed over. His skin was pale, and although she had never seen him before, the unnatural color proved to be far from normal. She watched as the fierce wind puppeteered his body as if to taunt her, demonstrating the power that it had. The rope creaked at the branch as though the wood was moaning his mourning. A flash of the full moon through the clouds illuminated the contours of his face. She was surprised that she could even see his face at all. The creatures had not touched his body and now Clara could swear that she had more blood on her than the body, despite her lack of encounter. They were not hungry.

She wondered what could have led this young man to the woods and convinced him to hang the noose. What was it that his now unblinking eyes saw that allowed his head to enter the loop as though it was a portal into a brighter dimension? She wondered if they could still see them in their petrified state, but only saw the moon reflected in their orbs. She considered cutting the body down from the branch, but decided that there was nothing to gain from such an act and knew that, regardless of the horrors she was coming across, she had to endeavor until she escaped the woods.

She decided she would walk, no, run beside the stream, understanding that the three bodies she had discovered had all been around the trees. Perhaps a change in scenery would yield different results. The myths did tell of vitality at the stream, after all. She knew she would be able to follow downstream until she was free. And so she set off on her path, her heart firing away as though it would abandon her at any second. Still, she endeavored, hoping she would find some solace at some point in her life. She thought to herself that she should probably remain optimistic but knew that after these events, she would need a lot of psychological help. She decided it would be best to leave that help for the future and put all of her focus into the present.

The rain was crystallizing into snow by now, each flake clouding her vision more and more, and a thin film beginning to cover the stream. She hoped that she would still be able to identify the path of the stream, should the snow cover it in the same thickness as land, but decided she would worry about that when the time came. The snow was definitely sticking, however, causing her to accelerate, her boots crunching with the impact. She fell into a rhythm, the cardio warming her body despite the freezing temperatures around her, until she spotted something strange emerging from the stream.

As she approached it, she held her breath, hoping it wouldn't be what she feared. Unfortunately, it was. The torso of an older woman had washed up onto the riverbank and frozen with the rain. She was covered in gashes that had frosted over, and snow was beginning to settle in her hair as if to taunt her. Her skin, now waterlogged, was swollen as though it was trying to drink the entire river around it in gluttony, desperate for an antidote. Perhaps the odd qualities of the river would heal the wounds in her body. Perhaps she sought for it to heal her heart. But even in the swollen, gushy state she was in, she was completely frozen as though she was expecting to be thawed out in a new tomorrow. Cryogenics. Her eyes were closed, and much like the boy hanging from the trees, she appeared to be in complete peace, despite the conditions of her body. It was as though the world around her was suggesting the answer to be within death.

Part of her wanted it, but she knew how devastated her father would be if she never returned. What would he do with his life? How long would he wait for her arrival before giving up? She imagined a man like him would never stop believing, leaving her room and all of her belongings just as she had left them in anticipation of her return. She wouldn't let this happen. She had to see her father. And so, she continued to endeavor.

She was sprinting at this point, no longer caring about what she would see or who she would see, and allowed her determination to guide her as she attempted to escape these woods.

"Clara!" a voice called. She knew that voice. She knew who it belonged to. But she also knew what Doug and the old man had told her about the creatures within the woods. "Clara!" Should she listen? She ran faster. She refused to wonder whether she overexerted her body. She didn't care. She needed her feet to carry her. "Clara!" it continued. Would they meet again? Her heart dropped into her stomach. She knew what she wanted. She knew what she needed. Lust, greed, wrath– she knew not which sin guided her most. She saw a break in the trees in the distance. She had to make it.

Flash. She saw the pools of crimson surrounding Doug's body as if to flood the forest. Flash. She saw the explosion of the old man's detritis. Flash. The young man swung in the breeze, and the creak of the rope thundered in her ears. He was too young. Flash. A woman preserved in cryogenics. She needed to be okay. She needed to survive. She refused to consider what sort of fate awaited her if she continued in the woods. Flash. "Clara!"

The weather began to lighten up, and between the bodies of the trees came a bright light. It called to her and she felt it beginning to warm. The voice continued to call to her. "Clara," it sang. The voice sounded like music.

She saw arms reaching towards her. Should she run towards them?

It began to smell like oranges.

*And so, I yearn for the day on which we will find our feet
on the dusty surface of the moon.*

Yours truly,

Howard Lewis

END